Highland
Izzy Hur

© Izzy Hunter, 2018

This is a work of fiction. Similarities to real people, places, or events are entirely coincidental.
Visit Three Headed Writer[1] for more titles from the author.

1. https://www.threeheadedwriter.weebly.com

Also by Izzy Hunter

CHAPTER ONE

The sandy-haired highlander bound into the simple, eighteenth century scottish dwelling, where a bright-eyed woman stood, hand clutched to bosom with anticipation.

"I've loved ye from afar," he said, with a low burr. "Now is the time I must act upon my feelings and, swear to ye, my love, that I cannae live without ye." As he pulled her to him, her breath caught in her throat.. "Just one wee kiss is all I ask of ye." He cupped her face between weather-worn hands.

"Oh yes..." Her eyes fluttered shut, the gap between them closing.

As they kissed, the woman's hands travelled south towards the folds of his kilt in search of further intimacy. Her beloved stepped back from the clinch, red-faced.

"I must away, my love. Take this as a token of my affection for ye." He delved into the folds of the kilt and produced a single white rose. The woman accepted it and gazed back at him with dilated eyes. Under his spell.

Reaching out to stroke her face once more, the highlander left the humble dwelling. The woman sniffed the flower, then dropped onto the bed with a look of longing...

The cameras stopped rolling. Half a mile away, in a building overlooking the Scottish countryside, the screen before me turned black. The number one rule at *Highland Fling*: No filming to be undertaken when the client is alone after dark.

I placed the headset on the desk and shut down the computer. Another day over. Now bed was calling.

Gemma Strong strolled along the corridor as I left my office. "Coming to the pub, Carla?"

"Not tonight, Gem. Too tired." I checked my handbag, making sure I had my phone and house key.

Gemma checked her watch. "It's only half eight. Surely you can come for one?"

"Nah. Maybe next time. Anyway, you're not finished yet, are you?"

"No. Still have to help Lance out of his garments." She raised her eyebrows in a suggestive manner..

"It's a dirty job but someone's got to do it, huh?" I teased.

Gemma pretended to fan herself. "Oh, you have no idea."

Someone stepped into the corridor behind Gemma.

"Oh, hi Lance," I said, as Gemma became flustered and spun to face the man.

"You did well tonight." She beamed.

"Thanks." The Australian looked great in the old kilt and shirt combo. The Scottish accent I'd heard through the monitor earlier, faultless. "You girls going to the pub later?"

"I am," Gemma blurted. "We could head there together, if you like."

Lance grinned. "Sure thing, sweetheart." He winked before passing us both and walking into one of the dressing rooms.

"Be still my beating heart," Gemma gasped.

"Now, now Gem. You know romances between colleagues aren't encouraged here."

"Who said anything about romance?" She wiggled her eyebrows again and then disappeared into the room after Lance.

I zipped up my jacket, ready for the fifteen minute trek back to the cottage. With summer now a distant memory, the autumn had brought with it an onslaught of rain that day which showed no sign of stopping.

Someone else was leaving Highland Fling HQ. Pete had been an assistant news editor at the BBC decades ago. Now he edited footage of fake romances for wealthy fans of highland romance novels. We'd bonded over a shared cynicism about true love. A three-time divorcee, he had sworn off marriage.

"Coming to the pub?" he said, sticking his black beanie hat over his mane of grey-streaked hair as we left the warmth of the building.

"Nah," I said, pulling my collar tight around my neck. I needed to hunt out my hat, gloves and scarf for tomorrow.

"Oh, go on. Just one. I'll pay."

"*You'll* pay? Are you feeling alright, Pete?"

"Oh, ha-bloody-ha. Didn't I tell you I won the lottery last week?"

"No. How much? Enough for you to become my sugar daddy?" I teased, and linked arms with him as we set off through the small car park.

"If twenty-five quid is enough for you, yes," he responded.

"Twenty-five pounds and you've not spent it yet?" I asked, feigning shock. "I thought you would have wasted it on loose cars and fast women."

"Pfft," he said. "What would I want with either of those?"

"Well, to date the cars and drive the women, of course," I responded.

"Been there, done that."

We reached the edge of the car park. The winding road out led past the village of Auchtermachen where the pub sat pride of place in the centre. The grassy path to our right would take me to my cottage. To my warm and cosy bed.

"Okay," I said. "Just one drink. And you can walk me back home, too."

"Deal," the older man said with a smile.

I grabbed the last empty table at the pub, unfortunately sitting by the door to the men's toilets. Pete went to the bar. He knew my tipple, so I swerved and ducked my way over and claimed the table before anyone else could.

I appreciated the log fire blazing away on the far wall, as I took off my coat and looked around the crowded pub. Some faces I recognised, others unfamiliar to me. A group of rowdy men played darts in the corner opposite.

There was a commotion coming from the other end of the bar. The Thistled Inn was an inn in the traditional sense of the word, with three small rooms for weary travellers. One such traveller had descended the steep staircase and was trying to weave her way through the throng of drinkers, towing a bright pink suitcase on wheels. I peered at the woman wrapped in a big beige jacket, and recognised her as Magda Churlish, a successful insurance broker. A secret romance reader, she had been one of Highland Fling's very first customers. And having just been with us for the seventh time, she was fast becoming our most regular customer, too.

She had just reached the door, when she turned to wave goodbye to Pat, who was now serving Pete. Her eyes scanned the room one final time, and that's when she locked eyes with me. I gave her a smile and a wave, but that wasn't enough for Magda. By the time she reached me, her suitcase had driven over several people's feet.

"Is that you off now, Magda?" I asked.

"Sadly yes," she answered, leaning on the handle of her suitcase. "Back to the daily grind. I wanted to thank you for the superb week. Lance was gorgeous!"

We tried to keep an air of mystery surrounding the Highland Heartthrobs. And that included not telling the clients their real names. What else had the antipodean been revealing?

"Glad you had fun," I said instead.

"Oh, I always do. Yes, I'll be sad to see him go. I'm sure the other boys will be just as lovely."

"Mm. Wait, what? Who's going?" I asked.

"Lance. You didn't know?"

"Well I do, now. What did he say?" This was ridiculous. Not only was he giving clients his real name, he was also breaking character in their presence.

"He said he'd been looking for work in one of the cities for a while. Applied for a restaurant manager job in Glasgow and got it."

"When exactly was he going to tell us?" I said out loud though it wasn't particularly directed at Magda.

"Oh dear, have I got him into trouble?" Magda asked.

"No." Well, maybe.

Pete arrived with our drinks, and exchanged a brief hello with Magda..

"Anyway," Magda continued. "I'm off to Inverness now, and then travelling to Birmingham in the morning."

"Have a safe journey," I called out as she took hold of her suitcase handle and moved off to the door, leaving more runover feet in her wake.

"They're filming scenes for a movie nearby, apparently." Pete nodded towards the crowd. "They're the crew."

"Did you know Lance is leaving?" I asked.

"I'd heard he was looking for something. He found it?"

"Seems so. Why didn't I know about this?" My role in Highland Fling was officially 'Production Assistant, so I generally got to hear the gossip fairly early.

"I don't think he wanted to tell you," Pete said.

"Why not? What did he think I'd do? I'd have found out, eventually."

"He didn't want to hurt you, apparently."

"Hurt me? I'm annoyed that we have to recruit again. Remember the trouble we had recruiting the Heartthrobs in the first place?"

Pete leant towards me and spoke in a quiet voice even though no one could hear him. "He reckons you fancy him."

I was glad I wasn't mid-drink, as I burst out laughing. "What? That's ridiculous!"

"So you don't?." Pete was looking at me with curiosity.

I shook my head vigorously. "Hell no."

" I thought as much."

"I mean, yes, he's good-looking, but he's a bit up himself."

"God's gift?"

"Yeah. Him and Gemma should be here soon. She's welcome to him." I shuddered.

"Hmm. Gemma. I sometimes think you have to be oversexed to work for Highland Fling. Everybody's at it."

"Not me," I said, and raised my glass of Irish whisky in a toast, before taking another sip.

"You mean you've not succumbed to one of the hot Heart-throbs?" Pete asked.

"Not my type. Long hair, bulging -" I paused for effect. " -bi-ceps," I finished with a grin.

Pete pretended to straighten an invisible tie. "Oh, so there's hope for me yet, eh?"

"You'll be first in the queue." I winked.

We finished our drinks and left. It was standing room only in the pub. As we reached the door, I saw Gemma and Lance standing a few feet away, pressed close together and not mind-ing one bit. Lance was saying something in her ear, and Gemma was giggling.

"Do you think they're sleeping together, Lance and Gem-ma?" I asked Pete as we made our way along the road.

"I'd bet money on it," came the reply as we linked arms. "Awful woman."

I said nothing. Being a friend of both I didn't want to side with one over the other. Gemma had no time for Pete. Part of me wondered if Pete was thirty years younger and had a six-pack would Gemma have dismissed him so quickly.

"So I guess we'll be on a recruitment drive, then? To replace Lance," I said, my breath rising in wisps before me.

"It's alright," Pete patted my hand. "I'll hunt out my kilt."

"Maybe we *should* have older Heartthrobs," I mused.

"I was only joking! I don't think my heart could cope pre-tending to woo all those women."

It was my turn to pat Pete's hand. "Don't worry, I'd never put you through that."

CHAPTER TWO

Lance didn't officially hand in his notice until he came back from his long weekend off. Once a "romance" ends and the client leaves with their DVD and a smile on their face, the Heartthrob gets two days holiday to rest and recuperate for the next client.

In truth, being a Highland Fling Heartthrob isn't rocket science. They needed to be good at improvisation, charming, Scottish – or able to do a near-perfect Scots accent, and be reasonably attractive.

So one would think we'd have no trouble in recruiting people for the role. Easier said than done. Once the time-wasters and narcissistic posers were dealt with, we didn't have a big pot to play with. That's why the three Heartthrobs we currently had (including the nearly departed Lance), were from outside Scotland, and a little bit on the vain side. They were undoubtedly attractive in that muscular, chisel-jawed way, however, and had their charms. I pitied Terry and Tessa, the HR team who would have to search for Lance's replacement.

"We really need someone before he leaves," Terry was saying when I visited him and Tessa the next day. "What about scouring the modelling agencies again, Tess'?"

Tessa shook her head. "It'd never work. We need someone with some brain cells."

"That's harsh," I said, twirling slowly in Terry's chair as he leant against one of the filing cabinets.

Tessa shrugged and continued typing onto her laptop. I then remembered the fifty-something woman's last relationship was with a model for Abercrombie & Finch that ended badly.

"When's Lance leaving?" I asked.

"His leaving party's tomorrow at The Thistled Inn," said Terry, gently moving me off his chair. "We've booked the small function room from 6 pm."

"Tomorrow?!" I cried, causing the twosome to look at me. "He's away tomorrow and you've not got a replacement?"

"Calm down, Caz," Terry said, with a chuckle. "We've got a couple of candidates coming today and tomorrow. And we've already had some video interviews. The model thing was just a back-up."

"Three clients arrive in the next week. What if we don't have enough Heartthrobs?" I pressed.

"Freddie or Stefan will have to double-up." Tessa shrugged. "Lance has been covering for Freddie being on his honey-moon."

"When's the Fredster back?" asked Terry.

"I think they're landing in Glasgow tomorrow afternoon," Tessa said.

"We need more Heartthrobs," I said. "It's no good the guys having to double-up with clients."

"I still think we should have some women working for us," said Terry. "A lot of men read romance, you know."

"Well, you're more than welcome to branch off and start up your own business," said Tessa.

"Highland Sweethearts," said Terry in a faraway voice, warming to his theme.

Tessa and I shared a look. It sounded like a beauty pageant from the 1950s. Still, *Highland Heartthrobs* wasn't much better.

I left them squabbling and after a quick trip to the kitchen, returned to my office with a cup of tea. I had a visitor in the shape of Lance who was sitting with his feet up on the chair opposite my desk. He quickly moved them when I entered the room.

"Lance, what do I owe this pleasure?" I said, rounding the desk and sitting down, nursing my cup.

"I'm just doing the rounds," he explained, his faux-Scottish accent from earlier now given way to his original Brisbane brogue. "Guess you've heard I'm moving onto pastures new?"

"Yeah, I was just speaking to HR about you."

"All bad I hope," he grinned.

I forced myself to smile at the attempt at humour. "Your fans will miss Dougal McDonald," I told him, referring to the Lance's Highland Heartthrob character.

"Yeah, I know." No modesty. "They're having a leaving party for me tomorrow after work," he went on. "You should come, despite everything."

"I'll pop by at some point," I assured him. "Hang on, what do you mean 'despite everything'?"

I got a grin in response. "You know."

"No, I don't know." I really didn't.

"I know you fancy me, Carla. You're pretty. Not really my type, though. I didn't want you to feel awkward about coming tomorrow."

I was so taken aback that I practically barked with laughter. "What? Why do you think I fancy you?"

"It's okay. You don't have to pretend anymore."

"Lance, I really don't fancy you."

"Yeah, sure."

I set my cup down on the desk and leant forward. "Lance, I don't know why on earth you think I like you in that way. Hand on heart, I can categorically say that I definitely one hundred percent do not, nor have ever, fancied you or seen you more than just a co-worker."

"It's okay." Great, he didn't believe me. If *he* was under the illusion I liked him in that way, who else thought the same?

I tried again as he headed for the door. "Lance, I do *not* fancy you."

"Sure. See you later." He opened the door and was about to walk out when he looked back at me. "You know, since I am leaving anyway, we could always have a little -"

I didn't let him finish. Whatever he was about to suggest, I wasn't interested. "Bye, Lance."

He shrugged then left.

I sat there for a moment, wondering if the past few minutes just happened. Then I picked up my cup of tea again, replayed the conversation and laughed.

I arrived at the party half an hour after finishing work. I'd tried to get Pete to tag along, but he had band practice with the electro swing septet he'd joined earlier in the year, as a trumpet player. The group - *Edison's Lightbulb Moment* - had never gone public. It was little more than a hobby.

The party was being held in a large-ish function room just off the pub itself. There were already plenty of people there, throwing back alcohol like it was going out of fashion, dancing to some music I didn't recognise and chatting in little cliques.

Despite knowing most people there, in various degrees, I hovered near the doorway, giving the occasional acknowledgement to anyone who looked in my direction. Gemma stopped briefly to chat, however once she spotted Lance, she was gone. I watched her dance with him, unsure if she was tipsy already or if that's how she actually danced. She was boldly manhandling Lance who didn't seem to mind one bit, judging by the grin on his face.

I checked my watch after what seemed like forever and realised I'd only been there for ten minutes. I wasn't in the mood for partying so I slipped back into the main bar and took an unoccupied table near the fireplace. A book lay there. I looked around to see if anyone was heading back to retrieve it, then checked the inside.

This book is yours to finish. Please leave it somewhere so someone else can take pleasure in it.

Ah. I'd heard about this. A book was left in a random place to be read by anyone who happened upon it. Then once that person was finished, they'd leave it somewhere else for another person to discover. It was a nice idea, and I wondered how far the book had travelled.

It was a Robert Harris novel, set in Roman times. Having a vague interest in history, I thought I'd give it a go, but ordered a drink first.

Fifty pages in, I came up for air. I was enjoying the book so much the din from the pub had seemed like someone had lowered the volume. Now, it was full blast again.

I glanced across the pub, still hearing the raucousness coming from next door. Opposite, someone sat reading The Daily Informer, a tabloid newspaper full of unapologetic bullshit stories. I took in the latest headline - some Hollywood actress had had the audacity to age - and scowled. I was still scowling when the paper was lowered and I found myself face to handsome-face with the reader.

"Can I help you?" he asked. His tone was soft and his accent from somewhere in the south east of England.

I shook my head, smiled and focussed on my drink.

"Would you like a read?" I looked up. The man opposite was holding out the newspaper, now finished with and folded.

"God no," I blurted out, then winced at my abruptness.

The man chuckled and placed the paper on the table. "Not a fan, I take it?"

"Correct," I answered. Earlier in the year, the tabloid had slated Highland Fling in one of their typically uninformed articles. No one from the paper had even bothered to interview anyone from the company. The journalist had written their slanderous piece from the cosy confines of London. Mercifully, the article hadn't resulted in a drop in clients or interest.

Someone stumbled through from the party and headed to the toilets. As the function room door gradually closed, I peered in. People staggered and swayed to the music being played.

"Not going back in?' It was the man again. "You keep looking over," he added, on seeing the look on my face.

"Nah. Too much of a lightweight," I replied.

"Is it someone's birthday?"

"Leaving do." I cast a glance at the closed door again. "Talking of leaving." I drained the rest of my glass and stood to leave, slipping on my coat and scarf. I was planning to take the book home and finish it, too. As I stood there, slipping on my gloves, I sensed the guy watching.

"You're the only person apart from the barman that's talked to me this evening," he said, as if imparting an interesting fact.

"Are the crew not with you?" I asked, busy buttoning up my coat, ready for the onslaught of rain outside.

"Crew?"

"Are you not part of the movie they're shooting nearby?" I asked.

"No."

"Oh." I looked at him. "Sorry."

"No need. I don't suppose I can tempt you to stay. I've been told it's the highland way to buy a stranger a drink upon arrival."

I smiled. "Who told you that?"

The man pretended to think for a bit. "A stranger. In a highland bar."

"And did you feel obliged to buy this stranger a drink?"

"Hmm. I rather think I did." He smiled back at me. Tempting. So tempting. It was still chucking it down outside. Best to remain here and wait for it to calm down.

"Alright," I answered, trying to act cool. He was hot, with short hazelnut hair and big, earnest eyes. "Who am I to end your drinking tradition?" I sat back down and took my gloves off again.

He studied me for a moment, chocolate-coloured eyes twinkling, then offered a hand. "Jack."

I slipped my hand into his. Warm and smooth. "Carla."

"Carla? Really? You won't believe this but Carla is my most favourite name ever."

"Steady, Jack," I replied. "You're veering dangerously into cheesy chat-up lines."

"How remiss of me. I can only apologise and promise that any forthcoming chat-up lines will contain at least fifty percent less cheese."

At this point I felt a small thrill. It had been a while since I'd flirted with anyone.

Jack stood, and I noticed he was tall. Another tick on my ideal-for-now man list. Lord save me!

"What would you like?" he asked, getting his wallet from his back pocket.

I bit my lip from saying the first answer that popped into my head. Instead, I cleared my throat. "Just a small rum and coke, thanks."

He nodded and slid around the table. I caught a whiff of an unnameable but spicy scent as he passed and, yeah, I sneaked a glance at his butt as he walked across to the bar.

Behave I warned myself. For all I knew, Mr Sexy had a wife and kids tucked away somewhere.

CHAPTER THREE

Jack returned with our drinks and sat down at my table. In such proximity I could appreciate his features more.

Please don't be married. Please don't be married.

"So," he began, getting comfortable in his seat opposite me.

"So," I parroted.

"La Ti Do?" he finished, then laughed at my bemused expression. "Sorry, it's just something..." His voice trailed off. He chuckled. "It doesn't matter."

"Are you drunk?" I teased.

"Not yet. Just tired. I left King's Cross Station at 5.30 this morning. It's been a long day." He took a sip of his beer.

"Are you here on holiday?" I asked.

"Sort of. What about you?"

"I live here. Moved up from Edinburgh two years ago. The peace and tranquillity was strange at first, but I think I've acclimatised now. And Inverness is only a car journey away."

"It is a bit of a culture shock," Jack agreed. "I'm used to vehicles everywhere, traffic jams, constant chatter. It's like stepping back in time."

"Hey, we're not *that* old-fashioned up here. Some of us even have electric now."

"Next you'll be telling me you have toilets inside your houses."

"Toilet humour already? And we've only just met."

His eyes twinkled. "I like to make a good first impression."

"And what an impression," I said, making his grin widen. I laughed. "So what do you do?"

"Apart from get teased by attractive Scottish women?"

"Uh-huh."

"I'm one of those big bad Londoners, who earns too much for doing very little."

I held my fingers in the shape of a cross as if he was a vampire.

He laughed. "What about you?"

I hesitated. It wasn't that I was embarrassed by my job. It's just that once I told people, they either wanted to know everything about the company or made a face and quickly change the subject. I wasn't sure how this guy would react.

"I earn too little for doing a lot," I answered finally.

"Very mysterious." He leant back in his chair and studied me for a moment. "I think you have something to do with the Arts."

"In a way." I copied his position and watched him. He adopted a coy expression and batted his long, brown eyelashes. "You have something to do with... law?"

He raised his eyes in surprise. "Law?"

I nodded. "But I'm not sure which side you're on. Good or bad."

He picked up his glass. "Oh, given the chance I can be very bad."

"I can well believe that."

Our eyes locked for just a moment too long not to read anything into it. This would be the bit in the movie where the two leads realised there was a mutual attraction between them. I was the first to look away, and finished the rest of my drink.

"I really do have to go now," I told him, leaving the empty glass on the table. "Work tomorrow."

"I'll walk with you." Jack left his drink, still a good quarter-full, and stood up just as I did.

"You don't need to," I said, though I'd be lying if I said I wanted him to.

"Actually, I probably do," he said, slipping on his jacket. "I'm not 100% sure where I'm staying."

I couldn't resist. "That's presumptuous of you."

"I meant I'm not sure how to get back to the cottage from here. I took a taxi earlier."

"I could give you directions. It's no problem."

"You could, but it would defeat the purpose of finding a reason to keep your company for just that little bit longer. You can see my dilemma."

"It's certainly a conundrum," I agreed. I zipped up my jacket and then looked back at him as he stood there waiting for my next move. "Come along, then."

I was thankful for not having brought the car with me. Not only was there a glorious and calm, early evening atmosphere but I was with a handsome man. All it needed now was the swirling, soppy music and I'd be in my own Richard Curtis movie. I looked around to see if Bill Nighy was suddenly going to pop out from behind the bushes.

"Everything alright?" Jack had noticed me scan our surroundings.

I chuckled and pushed my hands into my coat pockets. "Yeah, just being silly. So, how long are you here for? I can't remember if I asked earlier."

"You didn't. I'm heading back the day after tomorrow."

"So a weekend break, then?"

"Hmm." He looked ahead, no hint of a smile or playful grin.

"Want to talk about it?"

"Sorry," he said, giving me a bracing look. "Just can't face going back home."

Ah. Was he about to mention an unhappy marriage? An estranged family? I stayed quiet and let him continue speaking.

"It's just my job. I only got into by accident. It was only meant to be for a few months after university. 10 years I've been there."

"Yeah, sounds familiar."

"You, too?"

"Not now. But when I was in Edinburgh, I joined a recruitment agency just as a temporary thing. Eight years later, I finally managed to break free."

"Life is what happens to you when you're busy making other plans," said Jack, quoting Lennon.

"Very true. However," I said, finding the nerve to slip my arm through his. "You're on holiday. Holidays are for forgetting all your worries and having a good time." I caught the grin on his face. "And now you're thinking about all the different good times you can have, aren't you?" I asked.

He laughed. "You seem to know me so well."

"I know your type so well."

"I'm a type? Intriguing."

"Let's just say your name fits you ever so well."

"Jack? Ah, Jack the lad. Really? Is that the vibe I'm giving off?"

Maybe I'd gone too far with the teasing. "Sorry," I said, slipping my arm from his. "I'm a bit rusty at this."

"This?"

"Flirting," I explained, my skin warming up.

"Oh, is that what this is?"

"Well, I thought so."

He gently took my arm and slipped it through his, like we were old friends. Now the F-word had been spoken out-loud, I was more self-conscious than ever. "Whatever it is, you're very good at it," he murmured in my ear.

I looked at him. He was already looking back at me. We'd stopped walking at this point. Standing facing one another, in the Scottish countryside, with the highland mountains standing as a backdrop, as the sun began its descent. It was the perfect moment to -

A loud toot startled us. We were standing in the middle of the road. I collided with Jack as I got out of the lorry's way.

"Tosser!" Jack shouted after the vehicle which was already thundering around the bend of the road and out of sight. "You okay?"

I laughed. "It was my fault. Wasn't looking where I was going."

"I can't blame you. Not when there's an adonis standing before you." He said this this with such a straight face, I couldn't think of a comeback quick enough.

He took my arm again, and we continued our walk, mindful of the road this time. "So what are your plans for this weekend?"

"I'm not sure."

"No plans to spend it with a Sassenach you've just met?"

"Um..." I said, bemused.

"God, I'm sorry," he said, shaking his head and letting my arm slip from his. "I'm not usually like this."

"Like what? Forward?" I teased.

"Yes! I'm just realising what a twat I must sound. I don't know what's got into me."

"It's okay." I smiled. Truth be told, I was enjoying his forward twattiness.

"It must be all the fresh Scottish air," he continued. "And your accent. I thought I could resist the accent."

"I could try an Irish accent, if that's any good?"

"The effect would be the same," he said, with a sigh. "I think I need to go before I embarrass myself even further."

"I thought you didn't know how to get back to the cottage yourself."

"Ah. Good point. I'll just not look at you until we get there."

"Why? Will you turn to stone?"

"No, but I'm struggling really hard not to kiss you right now, so I may give in if I make eye contact." He said... while making eye contact.

"You're right. You are a twat." I laughed and linked arms with him again. I caught him grinning as we carried on down the road.

We fell into a comfortable silence. While Jack was taking in the breathtaking scenery and making content noises now and again, I wondered if this guy was too good to be true; handsome, smart, witty and self-deprecating. I was sure there'd be a twist to the tale.

"This looks familiar." Jack raised an arm and pointed to a small cottage a hundred yards in front of us. "I think," he said, squinting.

As we neared it, he nodded. "Yes, that's it. Red door."

I let go of his arm as he retrieved the keys from his coat pocket and, finding the right one, slipped it into the old lock.

"Well, enjoy the rest of your holiday, and have a safe journey back to London." I stuck my hands in my pocket and made to continue along the road.

"Wait, don't go," Jack called out.

I stopped and looked back at him. *Please invite me in. Please invite me in.*

"Do you want to come in? You've been very kind, making sure I didn't wind up at the wrong place."

Yes!

"You're not a serial killer or anything, are you?"

"No, not unless you count the odd fly or spider."

"Hmm, it's a close one." I stood there for a second longer, then approached him. "You'd better stick the kettle on, then."

CHAPTER FOUR

The first thing that hit me when I walked into the open-plan cottage was a strong smell of aftershave.

"Wow," I said, wafting my hand in front of me. "Do you normally use half a bottle of aftershave in one go?"

"Sorry about that," he said, closing the door behind me and switching the lights on. 'There was a damp smell in here when I arrived, so I thought Hugo Boss would do the trick. I'll open a window."

He crossed the room to the bay window and pushed the handle of the window open. "Better?" he asked, as he slipped his jacket off.

"Mmm," I answered, and unbuttoned my own coat. Well, I was here now. No point leaving just yet. "So, not going to offer me a cup of tea?"

"I can offer you tea, coffee, milk. Or an almost-full bottle of Glenfiddich."

"*Almost*-full?"

"I treated myself to a little dram once I got here."

"Just tea, please."

Jack crossed over to the kitchenette, comprised of five old-fashioned counters, with a sink at one end and an old cooker at the other. The whisky was sitting next to the cooker.

"I bet you find this different from your London pad," I said, settling on the sofa and watching as he filled the stainless steel kettle with water.

"Well, I don't live like a king, if that's what you're thinking. I think it's charming," he said, looking around at the fading bird-patterned wallpaper and 50s-style furniture. There were a few modern items that looked out of place, like a large wide screen television opposite where I was sitting, and a laptop - which I assumed Jack brought with him - lying on the coffee table.

"Let me show you around while we wait for the water to boil," Jack said, taking my hand from where it was resting on the back of the sofa, and helping me to my feet.

"Will it take long?" I asked.

"It'll take forever," he said, and I was well aware that he still had hold of my hand. "I hope you don't have a bus to catch."

"We'll have to see, won't we?" I answered. "Lead on."

Still holding my hand, he led me across to where the kettle was beginning to shake. "First, the kitchen. I think you'll agree it has an A-Plus in old world charm. In here you will find feasts beyond your wildest imagination."

I pretended to inspect the counters, even running a finger along the surface of one and then inspecting it for dust. "Very good, Jeeves. Carry on."

We moved back to the living room area.

"This is the heart of the home -"

"Aren't kitchens usually the heart?" I asked him.

"Usually, but I am a single man," he paused, and flashed me a knowing look, "so this is the heart."

I nodded. "Very quaint."

"Isn't it?" He relaxed on the sofa, lounging with an arm stretched along the back. "And this is where I entertain the most important of guests." He patted the space next to him.

I sat down and settled. "Mm, very comfy." The sofa was a two-seater. I found my right side pressed against him. His arm was still resting behind me. I half-expected it to snake its way around my shoulder.

I was too busy deciding if I'd mind if that happened, that I only just realised neither of us were speaking. I turned my head. He started a little, caught looking at me.

"We're in a very precarious situation," he said, his voice low.

"Are we?" I matched the level of his speech.

"Oh yes. I still want to kiss you," he said. "Really want to, in fact."

I'd wanted him to ever since that moment on the road. I'd lost count the amount of times my gaze had sought that inviting mouth. I took the next step.

"Well, you keep saying it, so why don't you just do it?" I asked, in a murmur, as I leant in closer.

He moved his other hand to cup the side of my face as my body responded to his touch...

And then the shriek of the kettle broke the spell.

"Holy shit, that's a loud kettle," I said, being taken out of the moment. Jack, however, was not deterred.

"Yes, it is, but we could ignore it?" he suggested.

I briefly weighed up the options - tea or kissing - but Jack closed the gap between us, and I was no longer thinking about kettles and hot beverages.

His lips were soft and warm. I could taste beer and peppermint. We finally came up for air a minute later, with matching grins.

"Now for that tea," he said, and went across to finish the drinks. The tease.

Still basking in the small glow of the kiss, I slipped off my shoes and sat with my legs curled under me.

"There you go." He returned, and passed me a cup.

"Thanks. So, do you normally give out kisses with tea? Most people just offer cake."

"Cake is overrated. And no, not normally. So you should think yourself very lucky, young lady."

"My cakes aren't overrated. I make a mean victoria sponge."

"I would love to taste your victoria sponge."

I met his gaze. "Are we using cakes as euphemisms?"

"Well, I can't speak for you - no matter how depraved your mind is - but *I* was talking about actual cake." He took a sip of tea.

"I'm sure you were," I replied.

"Although if you were to offer anything else...?" He let the sentence linger.

I set my cup down and faced him. "I'm sorry, but that's rather below the belt." I saw the change in his expression. From smug to worried. Satisfied, I continued. "If you think you can just insinuate that I would give you anything of *that* nature, then you're sadly mistaken."

He set his cup down carefully. "Carla, I'm sorry. I thought..."

I held up a hand to shush him. "I only deal in cakes of the sponge variety. None of your evil pastry concoctions. If you want eclairs, go seek a low-down, root-tootin' pastry chef."

He picked up his cup again. "God, you had me worried there."

"Just keeping you on your toes. You were getting a wee bit comfy with the old innuendo." I took a triumphant drink.

"You said con*coc*tion," he sniggered, emphasising the middle of the word.

"And on an entirely unrelated matter," I continued, "do you normally have a tea break during a kissing session? Not implying that there *will* be any more kissing."

"No?"

"Can't guarantee it."

"Shame. Well, I'll still answer your question if I may," Jack said.

"Be my guest."

"No, I don't usually have a tea break, but I think we need as much energy as we can."

"Really? Energetic kisser, are you?" I asked, finishing my drink.

"Couldn't you tell?"

"I couldn't be sure."

"I'll have you know I've won awards for my kissing technique." He'd finished his own cup by now. It sat alongside mine on the table.

"No, they were just *Aw, at least he tried* certificates. They don't count."

"You're very cheeky, you know that?" Jack asked, laughing.

"Oh yes."

"And it's very sexy."

"Oh yes."

He watched me for a moment as if deciding on his next move. "I wonder if I can get you to say 'oh yes' again tonight."

"I bet you can't," I said.

He moved closer so that our noses were just touching. "Challenge accepted."

I crept out, not wanting to wake him. There's nothing as awkward as the morning after a one night stand. There was no need to stick around until he woke up, anyway. What would I say to him? "Oh, cheers for the great sex?" We both got what we wanted out of our encounter so that was that. I didn't have to think about Jack again.

Except when I got to the *Highland Fling* building and nearly knocked Pete over as I strode through the double doors, he took one look at me and said:

"You've had sex."

I stared back at him. "How do you know these things?"

"Confidence," he replied, as we walked together along the small atrium towards the lifts. "You have a certain confidence about you after you've been with someone. So, who's the lucky fella?"

"You can't remember? I'm hurt," I teased.

"Heck, if it *was* me I doubt I'd still be alive to brag," he shot back with a grin. "So you're keeping it a secret? And there I thought I was living a wild life through you."

"Sorry to disappoint you."

We took the lift to the second floor and parted with the promise of having lunch together. I made myself a cup of tea and then settled down at my desk for the day. It was only when I caught sight of my reflection in the black screen of my phone I realised I was still smiling.

CHAPTER FIVE

We found someone to replace Lance; a Swedish guy staying in Scotland for a year with his girlfriend. The girlfriend was studying in nearby Inverness so the boyfriend had applied for the position for "something to do". He was attractive and had a charm about him, but his acting skills weren't up to much. We gave up trying to teach him the Scottish accent.

Lucas lasted three weeks before his girlfriend found out what his job was all about and visited *Highland Fling* in person, to tell us all that her boyfriend would work as a prostitute over her dead body. Our protests that we were not a brothel and sex was certainly *not* part of his job description fell on deaf ears. The girl flounced out, followed by a sheepish Lucas.

Now we were back to square one and advertising again. Every day I'd ask Terry and Tessa if anyone had applied. And every day I'd get the same response: a shake of the head and a sigh.

"Looks like I'll have to dust off my tartan trousers and brush up on my Billy Connolly accent," Pete said, over lunch at Mrs Threadgall's Tea Shop, one Saturday.

"Billy Connolly's from Glasgow," I reminded him, and sipped the hot sweet tea.

"I don't think many clients can tell the difference. It took me ages to notice the differences between Glaswegian and someone from Edinburgh."

Come the following Monday, I returned to work ready for the week ahead. There were discussions about changing the narratives to which the clients found themselves in after 'time travelling', and we'd all been asked to input ideas. I'd spent the Sunday evening, slumped in front of the television and jotting down a few scenarios. There was a morning meeting at 10.30 so I had plenty of time to get a coffee and check my emails.

I passed Gemma on the way back to my office. She was clutching a coffee mug in one hand, and her head in the other. I asked if everything was okay.

"Was out with some guys last night," she muttered, wincing as she spoke. "Went to see a band in Glasgow."

"Glasgow? That's a three or four-hour drive! When did you get back?"

Gemma shrugged. "A couple of hours ago."

"You should have called in sick," I told her.

"Yeah, I would have done, but my girls are both down with the flu." By girls, she meant her fellow make-up artists. "Chloe's just phoned to say she won't be in, today, and Verity's practically got an entire box of tissues shoved up both nostrils."

"Nice image," I remarked.

"I don't suppose you have any Paracetamol or Nurofen? I've got a right bastard behind the eyes."

"Follow me."

I led her into my office and she slumped on the chair opposite my desk, while I scrambled around the top desk drawer, and took out an almost-depleted pack of Ibruprofen. "Any good?" I asked.

"Thanks, hun." She didn't look as if she was going anywhere so I went to get her some water.

"Heard from Lance, at all?" I asked, returning with a plastic cup of water. She gave me a vacant look. "Lance. You know, handsome Australian. Worked for the company until recently.

Did funny things to your insides every time you saw him. That Lance."

"Oh him." From her tone, I gathered she was over her crush. " No, I've not heard from him. Why should I?"

I hesitated before speaking further. Gemma was a funny one. Depending on what way the wind was blowing, she could divulge the most intimate of things. Other times, she took great offence at even being asked how she was doing.

"And no - before you ask - I didn't shag him. Not for the want of trying," she added, with a mumble. "Mr Floppy."

Ah, so the wind was blowing *that* way today. I changed the subject before she could divulge any more information I didn't need to know.

"I'm getting Pete's present in the next week or so. Do you want to come with me and help choose something?"

She frowned. "Carla, honey, what on earth are you talking about?"

"Pete's birthday. It's in three weeks' time, but I want to head into Inverness and find him something nice."

She rolled her eyes. "Just get him a bottle of Glenmorangie, or something."

I made a face.

She grinned so suddenly, I tensed up. "Are you two sleeping together?"

"No, that only happens in your dreams," I said, in an ultra-polite voice.

"As if. No, I'm being serious -"

"So I am."

"You're always hanging about together."

I shrugged. "So? We're friends."

"I bet he wants to be more. Dirty old git."

"I highly doubt it. Anyway, what do you care who I hang out with?"

"God, there are guys - *younger* guys - who'd happily chat you up, if you didn't have a wrinkly old pensioner glued to your side."

I wasn't sure what she was getting at. Yes, Pete and I were mates. We got on. So what if there was an age difference? There was more to this than Gemma was letting on. I waited, arms folded.

She seemed to deflate somewhat at my position. "Okay, so the latest trend is to double blind-date, and I need a partner. Female partner."

There it was. Her motive for having a go at a platonic friendship.

"Double blind-date? So, like a blind date but doubled, and -?"

"Can I explain it later? I really just want to get back to the dressing room, close the door and sleep off this hangover... in between touching up hunky men in kilts, of course."

"Of course."

"Thanks."

She left and I concentrated on the day ahead.

I caught up with her again when I stopped for lunch. It was a gorgeous day. Nothing beats the Scottish landscape underneath a clear blue sky, so I sat on one of the park benches five minutes away from HQ, overlooking the mountains of the highlands.

She was already there; sunglasses on, cigarette hanging out the mouth and with a sandwich from the vending machine sitting untouched before her.

"Can I join you?" I asked, placing my box of pasta and bottle of strawberry-flavoured water (it was one of my healthy eating days) down before she could reply.

"Help yourself," Gemma replied, taking another puff of the cigarette.

We sat in a silence for a few minutes while I busied myself unpeeling the top of the plastic box of the pasta and unfolding the small plastic fork that came with it.

"It makes it all worth it," Gemma said, with a sigh.

I looked up from my food. "Sorry?"

"All this." She waved a hand in the air. "The scenery, the calmness, the clean air."

I raised an eyebrow at this last bit. Clean air while smoking a cigarette?

"How did the meeting go?" she asked, paying me her full attention now.

"Okay, I suppose."

"Any good ideas, or were they all a variety of woman meets man, woman fancies man, man pretends to fancy her back but all the while is pretending?" This last bit was spat out.

"Gemma, are you okay?"

She pushed the sunglasses further up her nose, then leaned back. "*I'm* fine. It's all the arseholes out there that aren't."

Gemma and I had spoken before about her apparent need of validation from men. It had not ended well. Thankfully, she had been en route to drunksville at the time so she never remembered the conversation the next time I saw her. Thank goodness!

"Yeah, the meeting went okay," I pressed on. "A couple of ideas were good enough to investigate further. None of mine, though. Which is okay. I'm not a writer or anything."

"They were a lot better than the ones they chose." A shadow fell over my pasta, I looked around to find the table being invaded by another *Highland Fling* colleague. Hazel was from Sunderland, in the north of England, and was one of the company writers, and another whose ideas had not been used.

"You'll know, Hazel," Gemma began, raising the sunglasses so they sat atop her short red hair. "Have they found another Hunk yet? I've heard whispers."

"Chinese whispers," replied Hazel, peering at my pasta before looking back at Gemma. "They're going over recent applicants again. Choosing from the best of a bad bunch, if you ask me."

Gemma shook her head. "I can't believe we can't get anyone half decent. If only Lucas had stuck around. He was good."

"Good-looking, that's about it," said Hazel, bluntly.

"He didn't need to be anything else," replied Gemma.

"You know, if anyone said the same thing about a woman, they'd be labelled sexist." Hazel was a feminist with a lowercase 'f'. She and Gemma had locked horns before, but nothing major had come of it. They both enjoyed their nights' out and getting - then rebuffing - the attention of guys.

The following Monday saw me have a rare day off. Ah, a long weekend, you can't beat it. But since I had no plans, most of the morning was spent doing housework. Returning the vacuum to the hallway cupboard, I noticed on the landline phone I'd missed a call but the person hadn't left a message. Then when I went to make myself a brew before tackling a stack of ironing, my mobile phone buzzed.

Just had a guy audition for Hunk role. Hot, hot, hot! Fingers crossed! Gemma xxx

I started to reply when I heard the front door go. It was Bryan, the postman with a package. At last, my new router had arrived. The internet was sporadic up in Auchtermachen, but this modem was supposed to be the best for online *not*-spots. Fingers crossed.

Busy setting up the router (which took a bit longer than necessary), I forgot about my text to Gemma until the mobile went off again. This time someone was calling.

I hit *Speaker* and laid it on the coffee table, while I continued attaching the pieces to the black, rectangular box.

"Hi, Pete. What's up?"

"This lot, going gaga over some bloke."

"The one who's just auditioned?"

"How did you - ? Gemma."

"Yup." I smiled. I could just tell he was scowling.

"She was acting like a silly little school girl when she met him. I could practically see the drool building up around her."

"Nice image. So, did you get to see him?"

"Aye, I passed him on the way in. Nothing special. Has that pretty boy look about him that you women go for."

"Hey, don't tar us all with the same brush.".

"And he knows it," continued Pete. "He's got an air of arrogance about him."

"That's not a touch of jealousy I can detect in your voice, is it?"

"I'll have you know I have plenty of arrogance, thank you very much. Better go. There's an issue with the editing software. IT have just turned up."

"Oh, good luck."

Less than a minute later, my mobile rang again. I was Miss Popular today.

"Carla? Tessa here. How's your holiday?"

"Well, it's just a day off, but it's -"

"Good, good, good, good, good. Listen, I need you to do me a favour."

"Okay...."

"Wonderful! Now, Carla, I need you to run to the post office and intercept a letter for me."

Intercept a letter? Who did she think I was? James Bond?

"Tessa," I said carefully, "this is my day off. Is there nobody else you can ask?"

"Carla, it is extremely important that letter is not sent. You won't know this , but we had a gentleman audition for the Heartthrob role earlier on today and, quite frankly, he blew us away. The chaps and I have decided to give him the job. But there's a problem."

"You've already offered it to someone else?"

"Got it in one. Gosh, you're a sharp tool. A letter of offer was written and posted this morning, but we've changed our minds. We need to get that letter before it leaves the post office."

I already had an arm in my coat sleeve. "Okay, I'll go get it. Just tell me the name on the envelope."

As Tessa relayed the name (and the address, just for good measure), I dashed outside and took in the overcast clouds. Disappearing back into the house, I returned clutching my car keys and went round the side of the cottage where my clapped-out, red Vauxhall Vectra sat in semi-retirement. It was my longest relationship and my most turbulent one. It had cost me more, over the years, than I paid for it. Lots of people had told me to get rid of it, but it held too many memories for me to dump like an inconvenient boyfriend.

I couldn't remember the last time I'd used it, preferring to walk most places where possible. I wound down a window and started the engine, praying to the God of Automobiles that the thing would work first time.

"Come on, Iris," I muttered, after she gave a paltry cough. "I'll buy you some new seat covers." I turned the ignition once more, and the car spluttered into life. "Good girl," I cooed, and led her down onto the road.

It was pointless trying to find the post van, so I made my way straight to the post office itself and wait on Bryan's return..

The recently refurbished building had gone from cold, bad lighting and creaky cash register to modern, soulless and a MDF-clad interior - just as its siblings across the UK were going the way of the banks, or else be absorbed into parts of other shops.

I stood there, surveying the line of mostly pensioners. Being British, I was fully aware of the number one rule: never jump the queue. Get to the back and wait your turn. But this was an emergency, and I wasn't looking to give custom.

I could hear the gasps and tuts as I headed to the glass-fronted counter. I held my head high and reached Janet, the postmistress who was serving Mrs Rivers, a retired nurse. Both women paused their transaction and regarded me.

"Morning," I said brightly, then checked the clock behind Janet. Yes, still morning.

"Hi, Carla," Janet continued, tapping away the computer. "I'm serving Edith, at the moment. Do you want to join the queue?"

"No respect," I heard someone mutter behind me.

"I don't need to join the queue -"

More gasps filled the air.

"I fought the war for you lot," said the same voice from before. "No respect at all."

Janet leaned towards the glass. "Yes, but you didn't, Bill. You were born in 1951, unless your pension book is lying."

One or two people laughed.

"You *will* have to join the line, though, Carla. These people were here first."

"I'm looking for Bryan. Is he back from his rounds yet?" I asked.

"Bryan?" She looked surprised, and I didn't blame her. I'd never spoken to her husband, ever. Well, unless saying "thanks" when receiving my post. Her eyes narrowed. "What do you want with Bryan?"

"She maybe wants him to join the Highland Heartthrobs," squeaked Miss Longshaw, peeking over Bill's shoulder.

Janet made a face. "Do you want them to lose business? Ah, speak of the devil."

"What have I done now?" The man in question had arrived back at the post office, carrying his mail bag. He disappeared through a side door, only to emerge in the sorting area behind Janet.

"There's a young woman here to see you," Janet explained, emphasising the word 'young'.

Bryan frowned at me. "What do you want? You already got your post, don't say you didn't."

"I'm after a letter that was posted this morning," I called out.

"Pop round the back" Janet said.

I thanked Janet and slipped through to join Bryan in the sorting room. He was pouring that morning's mail onto a large table in the centre of the room.

"People who don't want a letter posted, don't usually post it," he said.

"I didn't. But I've been asked to retrieve it."

Bryan huffed, then asked for details. I told him the name and address.

"I'll keep an eye out while I'm sorting this lot out."

"Thank you." I stood waiting.

He watched me, scowl still in place. "Well, wait out there, then."

"Oh, right."

The queue had dwindled down to just Ms. Longshaw and Bill, who was being served. He cast me a dark look from beneath wiry grey eyebrows. I took a sudden interest in the display cabinet full of greeting cards to my left.

When the shop had emptied again, I was still there. How long did it take to find one letter? Janet disappeared through the back, returning seconds later clutching an A4-sized envelope with the Highland Fling logo emblazoned above the plastic window.

She passed it over. "Here you go."

"Thank you." I slipped the car keys from my pocket, ready to leave.

"So, why didn't you want it posted?" Janet asked, as I headed for the door.

"They *were* going to offer a job to this guy," I said, waving the envelope. "But someone else auditioned. They preferred him."

"Oh, one of those Hunkies, you mean?" She glanced behind to check Bryan wasn't listening, then leaned towards me. "If I had the money, I'd book one of your Highland Flings."

"We run competitions now and again for a free booking," I said. "You should try entering it."

"Pfft," she replied. "Me? I never win any prizes."

"Never say never," I smiled, and thanked her again for the envelope.

Mission accomplished. Now, I could enjoy the rest of my day off. But when I reached the turnoff to the cottage, I decided to continue on to the office and hand the envelope back myself.

I parked the car in the staff car park and, remembering to grab the envelope, then made my way into the building. I waved hello to Pierre, the receptionist, and took the lifts. I found Tessa at her desk, sipping a coffee.

"Did you get the letter?" Her eyebrows rose with hope.

"Yup." I waved the envelope before placing it on her desk.

"You're a lifesaver, Carla." She picked up the letter and tore it in two. "This could have been embarrassing."

"It's okay. Just slip an extra fifty quid in with my next wage." I was joking but Tessa just gave me a look. "Where's Terry?" I asked, looking across to the empty desk across from Tessa's.

"London. Cosying up to some marketing companies. We're trying to go global. So that means wining, dining and snuggling up to those with power."

"Well, if you don't need me for anything else, I'll be going now. Enjoy the rest of my day off."

"Are you not curious about the man who auditioned today?" Tessa asked, with a knowing smile.

I wasn't. No doubt he was just another chisel-faced, six-packed guy. "I'll see him when he starts. I guess the background checks will take a week or two."

"They're done."

This was surprising. I had to wait almost five weeks from accepting the offer to starting at the company. "Wow, already?"

Tessa nodded. "I've still to hear back from one but that's a mere formality. He starts training next week."

"I suppose you needed someone quick," I conceded.

"True. But we wanted him as soon as possible. Women will go gaga for him. I've got a picture somewhere," she added, shifting through her mess of a desk. "Ah, here he is." She found her mobile phone and tapped the screen a few times, then held the screen up to me.

A grinning, crinkle-eyed man was focussing on something off-camera. He looked no different to the last time I saw him. There was no mistaking it; I was staring at my one-night stand. Jack.

"Lovely, isn't he? Those eyes! I think he's got Italian blood in him. He's English - from London - and can't do a Scottish accent to save himself, bless him."

"I know -" I began, without thinking but managed to turn it into an "Oh?"

"It doesn't matter. One of the new narratives we're going to try out is the Heartthrob being a prisoner in England since he was a child and doesn't have a Scots accent anymore."

"Uh-huh." I leant away from the phone as if Jack was about to leap out at me. "Well, I'd better be heading back."

"Not impressed?" Tessa asked, looking at the image.

"Not my type," I said, as I headed out the door. Then I thought of something and paused at the door. "Is he still here?"

"Not *here*, no."

Thank goodness. Nothing more embarrassing than running into a one-night stand unexpectedly.

"I think he's gone back to his cottage," Tessa added.

"Cottage?" I asked, hoping it wasn't the holiday cottage. I'd passed it in the car on the way up.

"He was here a few weeks ago and rented Callum Jackson's holiday let. He's staying there again until he can find somewhere permanent. You alright, Carla? You look pale."

"Me? I'm fine. Just... tired. Right, I'm off this time. I'll see you tomorrow."

"See you, and thanks for helping."

"No problem," I said, before closing the door behind me.

I was not looking forward to our awkward first meet as colleagues. Would he say anything? No, I decided. He didn't seem the type to kiss and tell. It would be best all round if we pretended we didn't know each other, but as I approached the car

I got flashbacks to that night and felt my skin burn. Sliding into the driver's seat, I glanced at my face in the rear-view mirror. My cheeks had a reddish glow to them. Damn, everyone would know something was up.

I drove away from the office focussing on the fact that Jack had intentionally auditioned for a job at the same company I worked for. I never told him where I worked, or what I did. I remember that much. Had he found out? Discovered I worked for *Highland Fling* and purposely made sure he got a position there? Hell, of a coincidence, if not?

Dear god, was he some sort of stalker?

Reaching the cottage where Tessa said he was staying, I sped on.

I got home and made myself a cup of tea. As I waited for the kettle to boil, I talked myself out of my conspiracy theory. It *was* just a coincidence. An unbelievable coincidence, granted. Again, the memories of that night played out in my head. Jack had mentioned he was looking for a career change and had fallen in love with the Scottish highlands. Obviously, he had found out about the auditions, and saw that as the career change, and the excuse to come back to Scotland, that he was looking for.

I decided not to think about it for the rest of the night. I'd worry about it in the morning.

CHAPTER SIX

If I had to give the next week a name, it would be The One Where Gemma Constantly Talks About Jack. Lance had well and truly been forgotten as far as the makeup artist was concerned. Where the australian's photograph had sat on the wall in Gemma's room (for makeup continuity purposes, you understand), Jack's brooding face now looked out at the world.

Every time I saw Gemma that week, the conversation would eventually turn to the newest Highland Heartthrob. Other people noticed, too, and eyes would roll at the mention of Jack Jefferson..

"The woman's obsessed," Pete pointed out on the Thursday as we met up in the lunch canteen. "Again! First it was Michael, then Toby, then Lance and now this Jack fella."

"She's maybe waiting for you to ask her out," I teased.

"She'll be waiting a long time, then."

"She's not doing anyone any harm," I said, coming to the woman's defence. "We all have our crushes and desires."

"But we don't all go on about them," Pete remarked. "I mean, look at you and your mysterious man. Kept that to yourself."

I went to say something but he held a hand up in defence.

"I'm not having a go, and I don't want to know, if that's what you're thinking. I'm just saying that some people don't feel like they have to share everything with the world. If Gemma likes someone, that's fine. I've no problem with that. But if that's all she talks about -"

"The Bechdel Test," I said.

"Is that the thing about women talking about men?" asked Pete, continuing with his sandwich.

"Something like that," I said.

All week I'd driven past Jack's cottage to and from work, on alert for any sign of him Normally, I wouldn't take the car but I didn't want to encounter him and not be able to make a fast getaway. Yes, I was overreacting, but this had never happened to me before. The number of one-night stands I'd had in my life - of which I could count on half a hand - never involved them working alongside me.

I drove Gemma down to the village after we finished for the week. I was in search of chocolate, so needed to stop off at the supermarket. I readied myself for more talk of Jack.

"God, what a week," said Gemma, yawning.

"Yeah, it's been a crazy one," I conceded.

"Not long until your holiday, though."

I smiled. "Three weeks and one day."

"I've been to Spain loads of times," said Gemma. "It's fun. But not as fun as Vegas. You've *got* to go to Vegas, Carla. You'd love it."

"I'll make a note."

"Going by yourself? Or is Pete going with you?"

"Oh, ha-bloody-ha."

"I still say he fancies you."

I ignored her provocations. "There's a group of us that have been friends since school. We meet up now and again, but this time we decided that since we're all now single and fancy-free, we'd go on holiday together."

"Nothing beats a girlie holiday."

Reaching the supermarket, we split up at the entrance. Gemma headed straight for the wine section. I grabbed a wire basket and began browsing.

I rounded the corner, mulling over which pizza-topping I wanted when I came to an abrupt stop. Jack was just inches away from me, peering at the back of a pizza box in his hand. I about turned and went down the next aisle, hoping he hadn't seen me.

Peering between the gap in the shelves of the freezer counters I found myself staring at his jeans-clad bottom. I allowed myself a shallow moment to appreciate his derriere. A young guy in a sweatshirt and wearing headphones appeared at my side to retrieve a pack of frozen veg from the counter. He paused and bent down to see what I was looking at. I heard him sniggering as he walked away.

"Just move," I said, willing Jack to leave that spot.

Then another figure appeared at his side. At first I thought it was a girlfriend, but then I recognised the clothing as belonging to Gemma. Oh god, this was getting more awkward by the second. I tried to hear their conversation, but was too far away. I was getting looks from the other shoppers, so I straightened up, hooked the basket handles over my arm and carried on shopping. I headed away from Jack and Gemma, and continued my chocolate quest.

Standing in the confectionary aisle, I was choosing between two chocolate bars when I heard someone call my name. Gemma was approaching, clutching a bottle of wine. Thankfully she was on her own, and not towing Jack behind her.

He was walking next to her.

Oh crap.

"Caz, look who I've bumped into," Gemma said, grinning.

I could feel my skin burn as those brown eyes acknowledged me with surprise.

"This is our new Heartthrob," Gemma continued, as they both reached me. I noticed Jack had dispensed with the pizza and opted for healthy, ready-meal instead. "Jack, this is Carla, who basically does everything in the office. Carla," she said, with a strange look of pride, "this is Jack."

A quick decision was required. Did I let on that we'd already met? Or should I claim ignorance?

"Nice to meet you, Carla," Jack said, taking control of the conversation. He held out a hand which I pretended I hadn't seen.

"You, too," I said, before looking at Gemma. "I'm almost done shopping. Do you still want a lift home?"

Gemma shrugged. "What do you think, Jack? Home alone on a Friday night?"

Way to make it obvious, Gemma, I thought.

"Or is there a better offer on the table?"

"I don't know," said Jack. "Is there?" His eyes met mine again and my belly flipped a little.

To save everyone from further embarrassment and unnoticed hints, I said, "Gemma's wondering if you want to go for a drink."

I caught the woman give me a look but then watch for her crush's reaction.

"Nothing would give me more pleasure than the company of two attractive ladies for the evening," Jack answered.

"One!" Gemma cried out, then composed herself. "One attractive lady. Carla's got plans, haven't you?" She gave me a hard stare.

"Yes. Sorry, maybe another time," I said, thankful there was a way out.

"That is a shame," Jack said, still watching me.

I said my goodbyes, wished them a good weekend, and grabbed the first pizza I saw before heading to the till.

By the time I got back into the car with my shopping, Gemma and Jack were paying for their groceries. I watched as Gemma bagged up her purchases; Jack waiting in the queue behind her. He saw me look and raised a hand, smiling. I returned the gesture briefly then drove home.

The weekend seemed over in a flash, and the next thing I knew it was Monday morning and I would have to face Jack again. I'd tried not to think about him and Gemma, and if she'd managed to get her wicked way with him. What concern was it of mine?

From getting out the car to reaching my office, I was on constant alert in case I bumped into Jack. I wasn't prepared, and wouldn't know what to say to him. Not yet, anyway.

In the kitchenette, I gave myself a pep talk as the kettle boiled. I was behaving like a child. No, like a teen and her first crush. I don't know why I was getting worked up over the situation. So what if he was working here now? It's not like I fancied him.

Okay, I *did* fancy him. Or I wouldn't have slept with him, but it wasn't anything more than that. If he wanted to work his way through his straight females colleagues, then who was I to stop him? I finished making my drink.

"You kept that quiet"

I jumped at the voice, then spilling hot coffee over my hand. I knew it was Jack, but I had a burnt hand to deal with. I let the cold tap run and stuck my hand underneath.

"Here, let me," he began..

"Leave it," I said, sharply. Then added in a softer voice. "It's okay. I've got it."

"You never said you worked here."

"*You* never said you were applying for a job here," I parried.

"It was a spur-of-the-moment thing, really," he explained, and broke into a smile. I bit my lip. He had a great smile. "I'd heard they were looking for sexy beefcakes, so naturally I applied."

"It's a long way from London."

"True. But I *was* looking to get out of the city."

"So you come to the other end of the country? You certainly wanted to get away, didn't you?" I turned the tap off and patted my hand dry with a couple of tissues from the dispenser on the wall.

"I like Scotland," he explained, then the wickedest grin spread across his face. Those brown eyes sparkled. "Besides, I have some wonderful memories of the last time I was here."

Oh god. I knew *that* conversation would occur. So much for pretending it didn't happen.

"Looks like you've made some more wonderful memories," I answered, still grimacing with the pain as I picked up my cup with my uninjured hand.

"What do you mean?"

I was about to mention Gemma when I stopped myself. *None of your business, remember?*

"Never mind," I said instead. "What are you doing here? Shouldn't you be having your induction?"

"The induction is at nine-thirty, but I got lost. I'm looking for Tessa Taylor's office," he answered, still glancing down at my hand.

"Floor below. Take the lift, then go right along the corridor and turn left. It's the door on the right."

"Corridor, turn left, door right. Okay, gotcha," he repeated, then asked again if I'd be alright.

I reassured him then headed back to my office.

"I didn't do anything," he said, as I was about to walk through the door.

"Sorry?"

"With Gemma. We had a few drinks, that's all."

"So?" My face felt hot.

"I didn't want you thinking I'm planning to sleep my way through the company. Well, the female section. Straight female section," he added, then grinned.

"It's no concern of mine, Jack," I said. "What you get up to is none of my business."

As was tradition at Highland Fling, whenever someone new joined, their first day would end with a drink at The Thistled Inn. This would usually involve the newbie's immediate co-workers, but for Jack's first day a lot of people turned up. So much so that - thanks to the balmy autumn evening - most people sat, or stood, outside with their drinks.

I hadn't wanted to go. I'd made noises about feeling unwell during the afternoon, but somehow found myself at 7.45pm that Monday, propping up the bar with Hazel.

Across the room, sitting at the table nearest the unlit log fire, Gemma was holding court over half a dozen people, and practically sitting on Jack's lap. He didn't appear to mind, at all..

"Do you think they've slept together yet? mused Hazel.

"Who knows," I murmured, feigning disinterest.

"Nah, I don't think so. Gemma would be all over him."

"Isn't she already?" I said, finishing off my orange juice.

"Ooh." Hazel broke her gaze away from the table and looked at me properly. "That sounded a little bitter, Carla. Not like you. Don't have a penchant for Mr Jefferson yourself, do you?"

"God no."

"Me neither. He's cute but a little on the young side for me. Give me Bill Nighy or Anthony Head any day," Hazel said. "Preferably at the same time."

"A toast: To older English gentlemen."

"Someone call me?" Pete appeared at Hazel's side, pint in hand.

"Now here's the very definition of the kind of guy I'm talking about " teased Hazel.

"I aim to please," answered Pete, and I could see his weathered cheeks turn pink. Hmm, that was new. Had I been ignorant of a crush all this time?

"We're talking about Gemma's new friend," I explained.

Pete glanced across the room. "Dear god, has she got her claws into him already? He's only been here a day."

"Works fast, does our Gemma," said Hazel. "She doesn't hang about."

"Evidently," agreed Pete.

"Talking of not hanging about, I'm heading off." Hazel finished the last of her drink then left it on the bar. Pat was passing on the other side and swiftly picked up the empty glass and took it away.

"A bit early, isn't it?" Pete said, his cheeks the colour of sliced watermelon.

"Work tomorrow, and I need to wait on a bus back home."

I frowned. "What's wrong with your car?"

"The brakes are playing up. Again. It's at Kevin Tait's garage, at the moment."

"Want some company?"

Both Hazel and I turned to Pete in surprise.

"No, I didn't mean it like that," he protested. "You'd be getting the number 62, wouldn't you?" He asked Hazel, then continued when she nodded. "That's the bus I get."

"Do you not want to stick around?" Hazel asked him.

He shook his head. "No. Two pints. That's my limit on a weekday."

"Can't I tempt you to stay for one more?" I asked.

Pete shook his head. "No, ta. I need change for the bus."

"Don't you have a bus pass?" Hazel asked.

This time his face turned crimson. Probably didn't want reminding he was of pension age, which was strange as he tended to brag about the all the free stuff he got since turning sixty.

"I can afford it, so why not pay? It's only fair," he said.

When Hazel went to visit the Ladies, I decided to find out what was going on.

"What do you mean?" Pete asked.

"You've blushed more times than Princess Di."

"It's a warm evening."

"And the rest," I replied. "Do you fancy Hazel?"

"Don't be daft." He fidgeted with the bottom button of his jacket, then added: "Anyway, I could ask the same you."

"Me and Hazel?"

A flicker of annoyance passed across his face. "No, Gemma's future husband. You keep looking at him."

"No I don't," I protested. God, had I really?

"Now who's blushing?" Pete chortled. He was probably glad to have the attention diverted from himself, but I had other plans. As soon as Hazel returned, I told her Pete had something he wanted to ask her, and left them to it.

I got accosted by an tipsy Gemma and found myself sitting opposite her and Jack. The others had drifted off. Now it was just the three of us. I spotted Hazel and Pete head outside. Pete caught sight of me, and discreetly raised his middle finger, I lifted my glass and grinned.

"So what do you reckon?"

"Sorry, Gemma, I was miles away. What did you say?"

"I was saying that Jack here is going to be a hit with the ladies, isn't he?" She had one arm casually around Jack's shoulder.

"Sure," I said, not meeting his eye.

"Was that Hazel leaving with old man Gandalf?" Gemma asked. "Has he finally given you up as a lost cause and moved onto some other poor soul?"

"Why do you call him Gandalf?" Jack asked, bemused.

"She has an aversion to using his actual name," I explained.

"So he's not a wizard who hangs out with hobbits?" Jack pretended to pout. "How disappointing."

"They're catching the 62 bus," I told Gemma, whose fleeting interest had already expired. "Actually, talking of Pete, I really need to get him a birthday present this weekend. Can you come with me? You're good at buying gifts."

"This weekend? Why this weekend? His birthday isn't until the end of the month." She sounded a bit defensive.

"I know, but I come back from Spain the day before his birthday, and I don't like the thought of all that money lying in my desk drawer."

Without warning, Gemma shot up from her seat. "I need to go... somewhere." She almost tripped over Jack in her haste. Then we lost her to the crowd.

"She's been on doubles since we arrived," said Jack watching her leave.

"She likes to think she can drink anyone under the table. Doubles means she's out to impress."

"No need to impress me."

"You two *do* seem to be chummy," I conceded.

"She's nice. Tried it on with me. Last Friday, after we met at the supermarket. Thankfully, I came up with an excuse to let her down gently."

So they *hadn't* spent the night together? That wasn't the vibe Gemma was giving off.

"You, in fact."

I was very aware of how close we were. "Me?" I asked, sitting back in my chair, intentionally widening the gap between us. "You didn't... I mean she doesn't know about..."

"You and I? Why would I tell her that? She told me about your rule about not fooling around with colleagues - and can I just declare my disappointment in that - so I told her that's my position, too."

"And is it?" I asked, keeping it light.

Jack leant closer, and said in *sotto voce*: "Depends who's asking to fool around." His hand rested near mine on the table. I tried to ignore the butterflies in my stomach.

His meaning was clear. His gaze spoke volumes. Not to mention he was now lightly stroking my hand with his fingers. Oh boy.

I couldn't stay here any longer. Iif Gemma returned, I'd have to watch her try in vain to catch Jack's attention. I stood up. "Maybe you shouldn't lead people on. It's really not nice."

I headed towards the door, but bumped into Gemma who seemed in a better mood now.

"You're not leaving, are you?" She asked, but didn't wait for me to answer. "God, Carla, I can't stop gazing at him," she went on, looking past me. "I think he could be the one."

When I got home that night, I stuck a ready meal in the microwave and then switched on the television.On screen, a man and woman were in mid-blazing row. The very next scene had the same couple in bed together. When the woman whispered 'Jack', I turned the TV off.

Okay, I liked Jack. But I hadn't expected to see him again, nor that he would end up working at *Highland Fling*. His behaviour at the pub could be taken two ways: One, he's just flirting (and you know he likes to flirt), or Two, he wouldn't say no to a second night stand. I have a rule about no work romances, no matter how much I like the guy. And what about Gemma?

She liked him, too. Yes, she fancies lots of guys, but she said herself that he "could be the one". Could he really when he's making eyes at me? And how would she feel if she found out I'd got to Jack before her?

CHAPTER SEVEN

Due to a full inbox, I spent most of the week cocooned in my office. I was thankful for the distraction. Every time I saw Gemma, she had a glint in her eye. And the odd occasion I saw Jack, his smile went straight to my belly and filled it with flapping butterflies. It was ridiculous. I was a full-grown woman, and he was just a one-night stand.

When Friday arrived, I was well and truly ready for the weekend to start. My eyes felt the strain from staring at the computer screen all morning. So when the clock hit 12, I stopped what I was doing and hit the cafeteria.

The place was already busy, but there wasn't much chatter going on. Instead, a gaggle of people were milling about the far side of the room, playing audience to a performance in mid-progress.

The star of the show was Jack (well, it would have to be, wouldn't it). He was wearing one of the Heartthrob shirts - a white/grey linen affair untied at the top to show a tuft of chest hair. He was currently undergoing an improvisation session with one of the dinner ladies. Kathy's hands were in his own as he attempted a Scottish accent. I moved off to buy a sandwich and a soft drink then spotted Pete in the audience. I stood next to him, watching the spectacle.

"Didn't think this was your cup of tea," I said to him, in a hushed tone.

"Oh hello. No, it isn't. Only came in for some lunch and caught this spectacle."

"How's he doing?"

"Okay, I suppose. I think he's been watching too much Pride and Prejudice. His speech is kind of stilted. Still, these lot seem to be lapping it up."

I realised the crowd was predominantly female.

"And his Scots accent is worse than mine," Pete continued. "They need to drop that."

I listened and winced. "Yes, it sounds more Irish. Northern Irish."

"Okay, okay, stop please." Glenda, the acting coach, stepped out from the crowd. "Thank you, Katherine. You can get back to work now."

Kathy smiled at Jack. "Oh, anytime." She winked. "Wait til I tell my husband I was wooed at work."

There was gentle laughter from the crowd as a few people broke off and went about their business.

"We need someone -" began Glenda, "someone a bit younger," she went on, in a quieter voice, in case Kathy heard.

Half a dozen hands shot up, with a chorus of "Me! Me!". I shirked away, but I could feel Pete's hand on my back, pushing me forward.

"Yes, Carla. You'll do, I suppose," Glenda said, grabbing my arm and pulling me towards her and Jack.

A half-hearted 'whoop' rose with one or two even applauding. I could feel my skin burn with embarrassment.

"Okay, just stand there and let Jack seduce you," said Glenda, taking a step back.

I wanted to die.

Jack gave me an apologetic look. It didn't help.

"Okay, Jack. You've just spotted Carla emerge from where she has 'time travelled' -" and here Glenda did the speech mark sign with both hands - "back from the current day. You're immediately caught off-guard at her beauty. Just pretend she's a heavenly goddess."

"Okay," said Jack, a smirk threatening to appear on his face. Oh god.

"And remember," Glenda went on. "You're a 18th century highlander - lose the accent for now - so no contemporary references, please. The script you saw earlier, that was just a guide to the storyline. Improvise as much as you want."

Glenda stepped back into the crowd. Jack cleared his throat. Self-conscious was an understatement. I chose to focus on his left ear. If I looked into those eyes, I'd turn redder than a freshly-painted post box.

"Are you alright, lassie?" Jack began, keeping his London accent. "You look so very pale."

"I'm fine," I muttered back, with a shrug.

"Where is your chaperone? A young woman like yourself should not be travelling alone along this road, especially one so beautiful."

"I wouldn't call this road beautiful," I replied. A couple of people laughed.

This caught an already-nervous Jack off-guard. "Um... no," he smiled. "Nor would I. I was talking about the ravishing lady who was travelling along it."

"I can't see any ravishing ladies, here. Nor, for that matter, a road. Do you need an eye test?"

"Oh, a feisty little thing, are you?" said Jack, eye twinkling.

I shrugged again. "Patronising man, are you?" I asked lightly.

Jack laughed, and opened his mouth to speak but Glenda rushed forward.

"Stop, stop, stop!" She cried, flapping her arms. "Carla, dear, what are you doing? You've just time travelled from the 21st century back to the 18th century, there's a sexy highlander in front of you, and you're giving him attitude."

"21st century attitude," I replied.

"It's okay," said Jack, grinning now. He was enjoying this.

"No, it's not. Our clients don't act like this. Right, Carla, you're dismissed. I need someone else." Several hands shot up. Gemma went one better and nudged me out of the way.

"I'll do it," she said.

"Be my guest," I stood next to Pete again.

"You've gone red," he told me, as the performance started.

I shrugged in reply. Before us, Gemma was making up for my lack of enthusiasm ten-fold. I remained for another minute then left.

Later that evening, I was sat riveted before the TV screen, catching up on a crime drama I'd been following. Until Gemma turned up with a wine bottle clamped in each hand. I stood on the doorstep, a polite smile fixed to my face.

"Thought I'd pop round," said Gemma, barging her way past without being invited in. She paused for a moment in the hallway before remembering where the kitchen was.

I closed the door with a grimace, then followed her where I found her opening all the cupboards in search of glasses. Wordlessly, I opened the correct cupboard and took out a small glass.

"Ah, good," Gemma began, closing all the doors. "Just the one?"

"I opened a bottle earlier."

She popped open one of the bottles, regardless. "Not interrupting anything, am I?' she asked.

"No, I was just catching up on -" I began, but she swept past me on her way to the living room.

"Good, good."

I returned to my place on the sofa, and switched off the television. Gemma sat next to me, and contemplated the plate of chocolate biscuits on offer before plumping for her wine.

"So what do I owe this pleasure?" I asked, keeping it light.

"Can't a girl visit her best buddy, now and again?"

I knew we were good friends, but the fact she saw me as a 'best buddy' was news to me.

"Besides, I wanted to ask you something," she pressed on, looking a little nervous.

"Of course." I took a sip of my wine and settled back on the sofa.

"When I was acting with Jack, you know, in the canteen? Did I come across as, well, obvious?" I found myself looking at a self-conscious, vulnerable woman.

"Not at all."

"Good." She said, as if confirming what she already knew.

"But what do you mean by 'obvious'?" I asked.

"Was it obvious that I fancy him?" She broke into a nervous titter. "Oh, it was, wasn't it? I just can't help it. He is so hot, and cute. Manly without being too macho." She leant back on the sofa and actually sighed.

"He seems... nice."

"Nice? Jeez, woman, have you actually looked at him? Forget all the other Heartthrobs, he is going to devastate our clients. I'm so jealous."

It was time to tread carefully. "But you do know that it's frowned upon to date a colleague, don't you?"

"God, Carla, I'm not some soppy young thing. I'm not interested in candle-lit dinners - though I wouldn't say no. I just *want* the man, in a lustful, primal way."

I took another sip of my drink, desperate to change the subject. I really didn't want a reminder of Jack and my -

"Carla. Earth to Carla."

I blinked and looked at Gemma, who chortled and tossed a crisp into her mouth.

"You were in a daydream, just then."

"Oh, sorry."

"It's alright. I was just saying, I'm thinking of asking him out. Maybe try that new Mexican place in Inverness. What do you think?"

"I thought you weren't interested in dating him?" I asked.

"I lied," Gemma said, then hid her face behind her glass for a moment. "I didn't think I wanted to, but he just does something to me whenever I'm around him."

"Have you checked he's not married or got a girlfriend?"

"No, he's definitely foot-loose and fancy-free."

"Right."

"So, what do you think?" Gemma persisted.

I didn't know what to think. They were both adults and, yes, dating a colleague was frowned upon, but it did happen on occasion. One occasion even ended in a marriage that was still going strong as far as I knew. Jack wasn't mine. I hadn't been looking for anything more than a nice time with a sexy guy; a one-off. So why did I have this feeling in the pit of my stomach whenever Gemma talked about him?

"Go for it." The words were out my mouth before I could stop myself. "But watch you don't get hurt."

"Why on earth would I get hurt?" Gemma asked. "It's not like I want to marry the guy."

I shrugged my shoulders, taking an interest in the biscuits. I felt Gemma's eyes burn through me.

"You fancy him, too, don't you?" she asked. Not in an accusing manner. More a consoling way.

"God, no," I said.

"Yes, you do. Why wouldn't you? Just don't get in the way," she added, in a jokey voice.

"I have no intention to. Anyway, are you still coming with me to get Pete's present at the weekend?" I added, relieved I'd found a change of topic.

"Yeah, whatever," Gemma replied, without much enthusiasm, though I noticed she was refilling her glass dangerously close to the rim.

Days later I was at work, searching of Gemma. One of the her silver hoop earrings had fell off during her visit and got lodged between the cushions of the sofa. I'd spotted it half an hour after she'd left, but the next day she had called in sick. And the next day. And the next day.

I met Pete and Hazel outside the editing suite, chatting.

"Morning," I trilled.

Hazel turned to the sound of my voice. "Hi, Carla."

Pete's face turned pink. He stood up straight. "Morning."

"Do either of you know if Gemma's in today?" I asked, reaching them. "I've got something of hers."

"Yes, she should be in the dressing room," said Hazel.

"I hope it's not contagious," said Pete.

Hazel frowned. "She wasn't ill, Pete."

"She was pulling a sickie?" I said.

Hazel nodded. "Don't tell her I told you. She said she had to go to Glasgow. An emergency, apparently."

"Hope everything's okay," I mused.

Pete was less caring. "Man trouble."

"Aw, you're so cynical," Hazel teased.

I left them and made my way to the dressing room. I knocked once then entered, immediately wished I hadn't.

Jack stood in the middle of the room, with his back to me, dressed in his Highland Heartthrob costume. Kilt raised at the front, someone knelt before him. I recognised Gemma's pink trainers.

Jack twisted his head and gave me a smile. "Hi."

Gemma leant to her left, and I felt reassured when I spotted the pins sticking out between her teeth. She took them out. "Oh, hi, Carla. Bit busy at the moment."

"The kilt's a bit on the long side. Gemma's taking it up," explained Jack.

"I just came by to give you your earring," I told Gemma as she got to her feet. "You dropped it the other night."

"Thanks." She stood there, making no attempt to take the earring I was holding out to her. I placed it down on the glass coffee table. I got the feeling she didn't want me hanging around.

"Well, I'll leave you to it," I said, and headed towards the door. "Oh, Gemma. Time's ticking, so I need an answer."

Gemma looked nonplussed. "Answer to what?"

"Pete's birthday present, remember? The weekend's almost upon us. I need to buy something by Sunday evening at the latest. You still want to come along? I thought we could buy the present then spend the rest of the day in Inverness. Maybe have a meal or something."

Gemma had gone pale as I had spoken. Then she became flustered and dithering. Most unlike her. "Oh, I don't know," she said, suddenly irritated. "You keep on going on about it, Carla."

"Sorry -" I began, taken aback at her reaction.

"I'll be back in a minute," Gemma went on, lips pursed. "Stay there," she ordered Jack, with none of the warmth she usually reserved for him. "I need to fix that bloody kilt."

Both Jack and I watched with bemusement as the make-up artist stalked out of the room.

"What did I say?" I murmured.

"She's been in a strange mood this morning," Jack conceded.

"Maybe she's still unwell."

Or maybe something happened in Glasgow, I thought.

"Right, well, I'd better get back," I said, realising I'd been staring at his clothed chest. "Just wanted to drop off her earring."

"Listen, Carla," began Jack, standing straight again. "I'm at a loose-end this weekend. I thought about going to the cinema to watch the new Hugh Jackman movie. I remember you said you liked his films. Don't suppose you want to come with me?

There's a deal on where you can get two tickets for the price of one."

"I'm busy, sorry. Pete's present, remember?"

"Right." If the disappointment in his face was an act, he would have won an award. "What about Friday, then?"

"Are you asking me out?" I said.

"I *think* that's what I'm doing, yes."

"Even though you know my views on dating colleagues?"

"I like a challenge."

"Why don't you take Gemma?"

"I want to spend time with *you*."

The butterflies were back. The way he was looking at me now was -

- ruined by the sound of a shrill phone going off. Jack darted across the room to where his jacket was hanging up.

"Bloody phones," he said, then slipped a small iPhone from his pocket and glanced at the screen. "Crap. I'm going to have to take this."

"I'll leave you to it," I said.

"Wait, what's your answer?" Jack said, torn between answering and waiting on my reply.

"I'll think about it."

CHAPTER EIGHT

After that, every time I saw Jack, he would give me a wicked grin. I have to admit it gave me a small thrill. Then I'd remember Gemma and the feeling would disappear.

I needed someone to speak to. To unburden all this on. So I called on Pete at his house after work one Thursday.

"Can I come in?" I asked, when he opened the door.

Pete looked surprised and unsure for a moment. "Uh, yes, alright. Everything okay?" He led me through to his living room which I noticed had had a good clean-up since the last time I was there. Pete's not a messy man, more someone who lives in organised chaos.

"Wow, you got the Queen coming round or something?" I teased, knowing full well he was anti-monarchy. Then I noticed what he was wearing. "You're looking smart, too. Going somewhere?"

"Um, no." He picked up an issue of *Record Collector* that was lying on the table and slipped it into the magazine basket next to his fireplace.

"You've got someone coming over." I concluded.

"Just... Hazel. That's all." Pete said, with an endearing stutter.

I decided not to tease him. The man looked so panicked. "I'll go," I said, with a smile. "I don't want to interrupt anything."

"No, no, you wouldn't be interrupting anything. Stay for a quick cuppa. She's not due for another half hour."

"Are you sure?"

He nodded, then went through to stick the kettle on.

"So what's up?" He called from the kitchen.

"No need to shout," I said, entering the room and taking a seat at the breakfast bar. I noticed the place had been cleaned and tidied to within an inch of its life. The man was out to make a good impression.

"Oh, sorry," he said. "What's up? You don't usually turn up unannounced. Not that there's anything wrong with that," he added quickly.

"I tried catching you before you left but you'd already gone," I explained.

"I finished early today."

"Had a lot of tidying to do, did you?" I joked.

"Oh, ha-bloody-ha. Anyway, you're avoiding the subject. What's wrong?"

"It's Jack."

Pete rolled his eyes and nodded. "You like him, too. Can't see what's so special about him, myself. I suppose -"

"I slept with him," I blurted out.

Pete looked at me. "Oh."

"Yup." I stared at a small cut in the marble top.

"Well, you're both consenting adults, I suppose," Pete went on. "I thought you were against office romances."

"This was before he became a Heartthrob. He was here for a holiday a few weeks ago. Remember Lance's leaving party at *The Thistled Inn*?"

"The one I never went to, yes."

"Well, he was there and we got talking. And, well, I don't need to say the rest."

"Oh, I remember! Yes, the morning after Lance's party, you came into work all aglow. I said you'd had -"

"Yes, well, it was Jack."

Pete finished the drinks then sat down next to me as we sipped our tea. "So what exactly is the problem? He's not hassling you, is he?"

"No, not at all. He's dropped hints that he might still be interested in me."

"But you're not interested in him?"

"I... I don't know. I mean, there's a reason I'm against office romances. If they end badly, it becomes awkward."

"Sounds like you're thinking the worst before anything even happens."

"And then there's Gemma," I went on, gazing at the wisps of steam rising from my cup. "She likes Jack."

"That's hardly surprising, She likes any man with a postcode."

"She's not *that* bad," I said.

"Maybe not, but she liked Lance, too, and now you don't hear a peep about him from her. And before Lance there was Thom, and before that Callum."

"He's asked me to go to the cinema with him tomorrow night."

"And?"

"I said I'd think about it."

"And have you?"

"Still am."

Pete sat upright on his seat. "Go for it, I say."

I looked at him. "Really?"

"Life's too short. You're not accepting marriage from the man. It's just a trip to the cinema. You don't have to go out with him again after that, if you don't want to."

I smiled at him. "I guess Hazel's mellowed your outlook in life."

At the mention of her name, Pete glanced at the clock on the wall opposite. "Don't be silly."

"It's okay. I'll finish this then leave," I told him, not taking offence.

"No, it's alright," he said, half-heartedly.

I downed the rest of the tea, thanked him for his pearls of wisdom, then left.

The next morning when I entered the building, Gemma cornered me.

"Carla, glad I caught you," she began, pushing a pair of oversized sunglasses onto her head. "I can't go shopping with you at the weekend. Something's come up."

"Oh, nothing bad I hope."

"Not at all. I just... need to be somewhere. Listen, we still have plenty of time to get him something. Why don't we leave it until next weekend, eh? I mean, there'll probably be lots of sales on. Why pay full price for something when we can get it cheaper a week later?"

"I know, but I'm going on holiday, remember? I wanted to get it before I left."

"I can get something for you. Don't worry about that.

"Are you sure?"

We reached the lifts and got in. I pressed *2* for Gemma and *3* for me.

"Of course!"

"Alright. Thanks, Gemma. I'll drop the money collection to you before I finish up on Tuesday."

"No!" Gemma cried, then composed herself, with a small laugh. "I mean, I'll buy something and give you the receipt."

Something wasn't right. Gemma wasn't usually this helpful, especially where Pete was involved.

The lift doors opened again and Gemma stepped out. "Great, that's settled then," she said, looking too happy. "I'll see you later."

I rode the lift to the third floor and walked along the corridor to my office. But before I opened the door, I heard a voice coming from the other side. I paused and listened.

"- not yet. Everyone seems nice, actually. Can't find anything - Yeah, of course. I know. Yes, okay. Bye."

I pushed open the door and stepped in. Jack was pacing the floor as he slipped his phone into the pocket of his jacket. He jumped a little at my appearance.

"Morning," he said, a grin appearing. The stubble on his jawline suited him.

I moved further into the room and dumped my handbag on the desk. "Can I ask what you're doing in my office?"

"I wanted to speak to you before my first job," said Jack.

"Today's the day they're giving you a bona fide client. Nervous?"

He shrugged. "I'll wing it. Anyway, I wanted to ask you if you've had any further thoughts about -"

"I've had many thoughts about many things," I interrupted, powering up the computer. "Any thought in particular?"

"The one where I take you out tonight?"

I looked at him for a moment. "Yes."

"Great!" He beamed. "My last call-up finishes around 9.30pm. If we grab a taxi, we can reach the cinema before the 10pm showing."

"No, I meant I *had* thought about it."

The smile slipped a little. "And?"

"The answer's no."

"Ah. May I ask why?"

"Instead of going to the cinema tonight, you and I are going shopping for Pete's present tomorrow." The words were out of my mouth before I could filter myself.

"Are we?"

I hesitated for a moment before replying. "Yes, we are. Unless you have anything better to do?"

"Nothing would give me greater pleasure than going shopping with you," he answered.

"Sycophant," I teased.

"I'd better get ready. That kilt won't fill itself." Jack winked, then left.

I shook my head in bemusement as the butterflies in my stomach dissipated.

At noon, I bought two packs of sandwiches and two cans of soft drinks and went up to the editing room. Pete was busy editing Jack's first footage as a Highland Heartthrob. In the scene, he was meeting the client - a thin, waspish woman from Connecticut, USA - for the first time.

"That's for you," I said, handing over one of the sandwiches. He took his headphones off and paused the footage at a close-up of Jack's face. I tried to ignore it.

"Ta." He tore into the cheese and pickle sandwich with gusto.

"How's he getting on?" I asked, delicately peeling apart the cardboard and plastic covering of my own lunch.

"Not bad. There was a slight hiccup where he tried the accent, but I can get him to re-dub that part in post-production."

"And how are *you*?" I said, emphasising the last word with a meaningful look.

His greying eyebrows dipped. "I'm okay," he said, warily.

"And how's Hazel?"

His face reddened as he fussed over opening his drink. "She's fine."

"Have a nice evening yesterday, did you?"

"Yes, we did Thanks for asking."

I couldn't resist teasing him. "Having another nice evening sometime soon?"

"Decided to go out with our friend Jack?" He parried back.

"Sort of," I said, with a shrug.

"Good girl."

"So, all joking aside," I went on. "You and Hazel, just friends or...?"

"Mind your beeswax," Pete replied, and took a gulp of his drink. I took a bite of my sandwich, chastised. "We're just two friends enjoying one another's company," he said, avoiding my eye.

"Good for you."

"God, look at the pair of us. Where have the cynical Carla and Pete gone to?" He joked.

"We're being smothered in kisses by the soppy versions," I answered.

I left Pete and returned to my desk. He had a lot of editing still to do. By two o'clock, my inbox was cleared, and I still had three hours until clocking-off time. I made myself a cup of tea and clicked on the BBC news website. I closed the browser button after five minutes. Then I googled *ideal presents for sixty-something men*. That was a waste of time. Aprons, mugs and t-shirts seemed to be top of the list. Pete never wore an apron, he already had an army of mugs and cups and the same went for his t-shirts. Maybe I needed to ask Hazel. Perhaps Pete had mentioned in passing something he was keen on (apart from Hazel, herself!).

I wondered if I should just hand over the money to Pete. Then he could do anything he wanted with it. But it was always nice to get a little something to open. Whatever we got, if it came to less than what was in the collection, Pete would get the difference.

That reminded me. I couldn't remember the exact amount so, since it was quiet, I decided to count all the money and exchange all the coins for notes. Easier to carry that way.

I pulled open the top drawer of my desk and sifted through the old reports and various documents I'd used to cover the envelope with the money. I got to the bottom of the drawer but found no envelope. So I re-sifted, going slower this time, checking every single sheet of paper as mild panic set in.

I took the whole pile of documents out the drawer until all that was left was a pack of post-its, a three-quarters-used bottle of face cream and an old lanyard with the company's previous logo emblazoned on it.

And no envelope.

One by one, sheet by sheet, I put the documents on the desk, checking the envelope hadn't got caught in amongst them. But as I place the last sheet down on the pile, I let out a groan.

Maybe it had slipped down to the second drawer in the desk, but when I pulled it open I was faced with an old brochures for Highland Fling.

And no envelope.

After I checked every inch of the desk drawers, including the surface of my desk - just in case - I sat there for a minute or two, remembering the last time I had it. It was in the canteen, where Kathy and Roy had duly signed the card and added some coins into the envelope. I'd definitely taken it back from them because I remembered having a nosy look at the platitudes they'd written before putting the card and the envelope, full of money, back in the top drawer of the desk.

There was no getting away from the fact. Someone had taken it.

CHAPTER NINE

Over two hundred pounds collected for Pete, and all that was left with was a birthday card and no means to buy a present. This was not happening! I had another look.

Minutes later I was staring into space. I had managed to lose all that money. All that money that didn't belong to me. Oh god.

Who else knew where the collection had been kept? There was Gemma, who had been given the task of doing the collection before it had been swiftly landed on my lap. Had she picked up the envelope when I'd been having lunch? But surely she would have left a note.

I looked on my desk and at the several post-it notes sticking at the sides of my computer monitor, but they were all in my handwriting.

I leapt up from my chair, intent on finding Gemma. There was no use panicking if it turned out she *did* have the money. But as I stepped out from behind the desk, another name popped into my head.

Jack had been alone in here this morning. He could have had enough time to snoop.

Oh god, what if he had a gambling habit and had sniffed out the money like a police dog?

Get a grip, Sherlock, I berated myself. There was no point jumping to conclusions. First things first, I needed to see Gemma.

But before I could knock on the dressing room door, Hazel appeared from the other end of the corridor, leaving her own little room, and clutching a blue folder.

"Looking for Gemma? She's just left. For Glasgow, apparently."

Glasgow, again? "Thanks. She didn't mention anything about Pete's birthday, did she?"

"No. Sorry."

I sent Gemma a text when I got back to my desk.

Hi, G. It's Caz. Did you pick up the envelope with Pete's collection money? No worries if you have.

Yes, that's probably what happened. There were more shops in Glasgow. She would find something there.

I put it to the back of my mind and concentrated on the day head.

Five o'clock struck, and I was more than happy to leave. There's nothing worse than a slow day at work. Time drags on.

Instead of going straight home, via a quick stop at the supermarket, I ended up at The Thistled Inn with Pete and Hazel. I really didn't want to play gooseberry, but Hazel asked. I didn't have to stay for hours.

As usual, the pub was busy, with half the customers belonging to Highland Fling. But we secured a table near the bar.

Conversation started off at the recent celeb scandal in the papers, but soon arrived at work talk. It always did, no matter how we all struggled not to make it so.

"We should have invited the new guy," said Hazel, scanning the pub for Jack. "First proper day as a Heartthrob. He'll be in need of a drink."

"He doesn't finish til 9.30" Pete and I said in unison.

Hazel laughed. "Am I the only one who doesn't know his itinerary?"

"So, what's everyone's plans for the weekend, then?" asked Pete.

"Not sure," I said. And that was the truth. Now Gemma had the taken control of the gift-buying, I didn't need to go to Inverness with Jack. And damn it, I hadn't told him the change of plan.

"Not off to the cinema, then?" Pete asked.

I had no excuse not to, but I just wanted to get home, into my pyjamas, and veg out in front of the television.

"Ooh, the cinema - I haven't been to the movies in ages," Hazel said with a sigh.

"Do you like Hugh Jackman?"

"Oh yes."

"His new movie is out. Why don't you go tonight? Pete can keep you company." There's nothing like a little nudge in the right direction.

Pete made a face, but Hazel didn't notice. She was too busy looking at her watch.

"It's only just gone half six," she said. "What do you think?"

"Yeah, sure," Pete answered, raising his pint.

"Do you want to come, too?" Hazel asked me.

"Maybe another time, but thanks."

"Okay. Well, let's finish these," she said, looking at the orange juice she'd been on all evening, "then jump in my car. We'll go to the first available showing."

"Alright," agreed Pete.

They left me fifteen minutes later. I was still nursing my strawberry daiquiri when the door to the inn opened and in walked Jack with a couple of the props guys. I pretended not to see him as they made a beeline for the bar.

He would have to be told the change of plan. I threw back the last of the daiquiri and got ready to leave. I'd quickly tell him on the way out. Not give him enough time to say anything.

He moved from the bar, heading for the Gents. Now was my chance.

"Jack, hi," I said, stepping in his eye-line as he neared.

"Hey." The grin was back. "Was just thinking about you."

I ignored the butterflies. "About tomorrow..." I faltered, getting distracted by a sudden flashback to our night together.

"Ah, yes," he continued the thread. "I was thinking we could have lunch somewhere. Any place you like. I've not tried any of the restaurants in Inverness yet."

I found myself nodding while the angel on my shoulder rolled up her sleeves. "I'll pick you up at the cottage around ten-thirty."

"I look forward to it," he said, with a wink.

I left before the angel became corporeal and punched me.

CHAPTER TEN

I awoke the next morning to the sound of birdsong. It wasn't coming from outside, however. Rather from my phone - the day phones came with sounds other than shrill alarms was a godsend. I'd set it to go off fifteen minutes earlier, so I could lie there for a quarter of an hour and pretend I wasn't a slave to time. When I got home from the pub the previous night, I sorted out two outfit options for the morning. For once I was going to be organised!

Showered, I laid the chosen outfits on the bed. Outside was dry but cloudy. Scottish weather being unpredictable, I played it safe and chose my dark blue kick-flare jeans and a white vest top and black cardigan.

By the time I'd laced my shoes up, it was already quarter past ten. I told Jack I'd pick him up at half past!

I retrieved the dust-covered hair dryer from underneath the bed (I normally towel-dry my hair) and gave my damp locks a quick blast.

Hair done, I only had time to wipe some lipstick across my mouth and check my purse and keys were in my handbag before running out the door.

The butterflies made their presence felt as I drove along the road. It would only take me minutes to navigate the rough, winding road to Jack's cottage, but time seemed to speed up despite the speedometer not going 40mph.

He stood outside when I pulled up. Leaning against the front door, ankles crossed, head stuck in a newspaper. He looked up when I tooted the horn and smiled, folding up the paper as he did so. *The Daily Informer* again?

I reached across and pushed open the passenger door for him. He entered the car and set the folded newspaper on the dashboard in front of him. I glared at it as Jack did up his seatbelt.

"You look great," he enthused, settling in his seat. He leaned towards me. I awkwardly craned my head away, then realised with embarrassment he hadn't been after a kiss. He'd just been taking his arm out of his sleeve as he slipped off his coat.

I started up the engine again. "This? Just some old clothes I found in the wardrobe."

"Suits you."

"Thanks." I intended to return the hollow compliment. He *was* actually looking good. He *always* looked good. The bastard.

"So a day of shopping." He slapped his legs with his palms. "Sounds good."

"No, it doesn't," I replied. "I hate shopping. Sometimes it's necessary."

"Like when you're looking for birthday presents?"

"Actually, I'm not," I told him. "Well, I don't think so."

He looked across at me. "I'm confused."

So was I. "I *was* going to go shopping for Pete's present but I think Gemma's getting something in Glasgow. I'm just waiting to hear from her."

"Alright," Jack said slowly. "If we're maybe *not* shopping, what *are* we going to do? I have one or two suggestions."

"I'm sure you do. I thought I'd show you around Inverness."

"Does that involve looking for Nessie?" Jack asked.

"If I was prepared to drive to *Loch* Ness, yes."

"And are you?"

"Not on your life. Stick a toy dinosaur in a bath, take a close-up photo and send it that rag," I said, nodding towards the paper. "They won't notice the difference."

"You really don't like that newspaper, do you?" Jack said, in a bemused tone.

"It's racist, sexist, alarmist and any other 'ists' you care to mention." I wasn't looking for an argument so I bit my tongue before I could say anymore.

"But they have good horoscopes." He unfolded the paper and flicked to the page he was looking for. "What's your star sign?"

"Leo. But it's a bunch of made-up crap."

"Leo. That figures," Jack muttered. "Right. Leo. *Today you should throw caution to the wind and indulge in good food, fine wine and a devilishly-handsome Englishman. Especially the englishman.*"

"It does *not* say that. What about yours?"

"My star sign?" He scanned the page. "Ah. *Today you should throw caution to the wind and indulge in good food, fine wine and an irresistible Scottish woman. Especially the Scottish woman.*"

"Your star sign is?"

"Leo, as well."

"Then shouldn't you be indulging in a devilishly-handsome Englishman, too?"

"I need to watch my figure," he replied, patting his flat-iron stomach.

I grinned as we travelled past the buildings that made up Auchtermachen.

"Are you buzzing, or am I?" Jack said looking around. My phone had come to life on top of the dashboard, the screen flashing. "Want me to answer it?" His hand hovered over the vibrating device.

"Ignore it. They'll call back if it's important."

My phone went off another three times. After the third attempt, I reached across and glanced at the screen. All of them from Gemma.

"Someone really wants to speak to you."

"It's Gemma. I'll call her later."

"Ooh, maybe she knows we're together and wants to claw your eyes out!" Jack suggested.

"Over the phone? And anyway, you sound a wee bit enthusiastic, there," I said, slipping the phone back into my pocket.

"Two women fighting over me? Of course!"

"You have a high opinion of yourself, don't you? Maybe we'd be fighting over which one of *really* doesn't want you."

"You'd lose, then."

I was about to agree, but closed my mouth instead.

"Gemma, bless her, maybe likes wee Jack but -"

"*Wee* Jack, indeed."

He lightly slapped my leg. "Hey, you weren't complaining -"

"We're here," I interrupted him, avoiding his gaze.

Jack stopped talking and looked through the window as houses made way for commercial buildings. After paying and finding a space in a multi-storey car park, we went in search of a hot beverage.

I checked my phone in a branch of Costa Coffee. Jack had a loyalty card and needed one more purchase to get a free drink.

"She's left a voicemail," I said, looking at the flashing image on my phone.

I hit '3' and listened to the message.

"Carla, it's Gemma. I want to explain." She sounded out of breath. "I'm trying to find him at the moment, the bastard. If I knew he would do this, then I'd never have - god, I'm unfit! I'm going to join a gym or something. I - oh, what was that noise? Have I pressed -"

The message ended. I stared at the screen. What the hell was she going on about?

"Everything okay?" asked Jack.

"Not sure," I replied. "I'll call her back."

I double-tapped Gemma's name on my phone, then held the device to my ear as the dialling tone played out. I hoped everything was okay. Gemma had been acting odd. Who was she trying to 'find'? The ringing continued for so long, I was about to give up when the call was answered.

"Carla!" Gemma sounded too enthusiastic. Automatically, my suspicions rose.

"Hi, Gemma. Sorry I missed your calls earlier. I was driving. Everything okay?"

"Yes! Of course!"

"It's just that your voicemail..." I let my voice trail off.

"Mm? Oh, that. Don't worry about it."

"How's Glasgow?" I asked, deciding to change the subject, since I was getting nowhere with the current line of enquiry."

"What?" Her voice became cold. "How do you know I'm in Glasgow?"

"You told me, remember? Yesterday? That's why you couldn't come with me to get Pete's present."

"Oh yes, I do remember now." She said, then forced out a laugh.

"Actually, I wanted to speak to you about that," I continued. "I went to get the money we'd collected for Pete, and -"

"Oh god, Carla! I'm so sorry!" She blurted out.

"Sorry for what?" If she had gone and fixed up some silly double-date -

"I took the money." She sounded close to tears.

"Well, yes I assumed that's what happened. Glasgow has more variety of shops, so you can probably find -"

"No! I don't mean - I mean, that I took the money weeks ago. From your desk drawer."

"Why?" Already I was dreading whatever reason she was about to give.

"Lance." Gemma said, then let out a half-sigh, half-sob.

CHAPTER ELEVEN

"Lance? Look, Gemma. You'd better just tell me what's going on." I heard the sharpness in my voice, but didn't care at that point.

"Okay," she said, her voice breaking a little. I heard her gulp. "When Lance found out he got the restaurant job, he needed to put down a deposit for a flat-share."

"Go on." I hit 'speaker' and set the phone down on the table.

"He was skint. I mean, the man's always skint. But he didn't have enough for the deposit. I could only afford a hundred pounds." She paused. Maybe she'd expected me to remark upon this, but I stayed silent. "Then he asked about Pete's collection, said he couldn't remember if he'd signed the card. So, we went to your office but you'd gone home by then. Turns out Lance had signed the card already and given you some money."

Yes, he had signed the card. But he'd never given me any money towards the gift.

"We were about to leave," Gemma continued, "when he told me about the deposit. He was really worried that he wouldn't be able to move in before he started his new job. I tried to console him -"

"I bet she did," muttered Jack.

"Who was that?" The coldness was back in Gemma's voice. "Who's that with you?"

"Nobody," I said, slapping Jack's arm. "Just a nosy waiter. Go on, you were consoling him."

I listened, dead-eyed, as Gemma continued her confession. That Lance had asked how much had been collected and, on being told, joked he could borrow it to pay the deposit.

"And that's what exactly happened," I finished for her.

"He was very persuasive," Gemma went on. "Promised that once he paid the deposit and secured his share, he'd contact his family in Australia and get them to send enough money to pay me back. Pay you back, I mean. This was supposed to be done and dusted before you realised the money was gone."

"So why isn't it?" I asked.

"He's not returning my calls or texts, that's why," Gemma hissed. "I've no idea where he's living. I know where he's working. Disappears whenever I show up."

"She's been played," said Jack, with a shake of the head.

I hit him again. "Sorry, nosy waiter again. So, he has no intention of paying back the money."

"Oh he will," said Gemma, with determination. "Even if I have to storm into the restaurant kitchen and march him to the bank, myself."

"Right."

"I really am sorry, Carla. I never thought he would do this."

"You never thought?" The anger had reached boiling point. "Trouble is, Gemma, you never think. You catch sight of a good-looking man and you turn into this sad, desperate woman who does anything to get noticed." I grabbed the phone and glared at the screen as she was there in front of me. "I mean, did you think by giving him money that wasn't yours to give, he'd shag you as a thank you?"

I paused, giving her a chance to respond. When there came no answer, I pushed my chair back carelessly and stood. "Oh, so he did shag you. Well, I'm so glad you got something out of it!"

She hung up.

I looked at the phone in astonishment. "She hung up on me." I said, then noticed everyone in the coffee shop was watching me. Jack sat with folded arms and a small smile on his lips.

"What's so funny?" I snapped at him.

"Nothing," he said, and the smile vanished.

"I can't believe she gave him the money, just like that. My holiday's on Wednesday. I've not got time to scrape together the amount I'd collected." I slumped back into my chair. "Shit."

"There's nothing sexier than a pissed-off, sweary Scottish redhead," Jack remarked.

It was the wrong thing to say. My anger had found a new target.

"Jesus, is that all you think about? There's more to life than sex, Jack. If you're only hanging about on the chance I'll sleep with you again, you're wasting your time. You know what? Maybe you should sod off to Glasgow and use your charms on Gemma. It sounds like it wouldn't take much."

I picked up my handbag, chucked the phone into it, then strode towards the door. "Show's over," I muttered to my audience.

Outside, I started walking without any idea where. I turned my phone off; I wasn't in the right frame of mind to speak to anyone.

"Watch out, love!"

An elderly woman in a blue knitted cap and floral jacket had grabbed my arm. I looked at her in surprise and then at the car I'd just stepped out in front of. The driver glared and shook his head. I hastily stepped back onto the kerb and thanked the woman.

"You could have got run over," the woman said in a soft Inverness burr, as the car drove off.

"Yeah," I said in a daze, unable to believe I hadn't been looking where I was going.

"You alright, love?" I heard the woman say, but the green man had appeared on the traffic light and I was already striding across the road.

I tried not to think about Gemma or Jack, or what I would do if Gemma couldn't get hold of Lance. Highland Fling paid reasonably well, like many people my age, I couldn't afford to save for a rainy day. Savings was just something other people had.

I carried on walking until I found myself back outside the coffee shop. There was no sign of Jack. This annoyed me; was he looking for me or cut his losses and returned to Auchtermachen? I trudged back to the car park, regretting the entire day. Going by the clock on the dashboard, I'd been walking around for two hours.

Reaching the car, I slipped into the driver's seat and realised I didn't have Jack's number. Should I go looking for him or stay put and hope he'd find his way back? I wanted to get home and close the door on the world.

Tap. Tap. Tap.

His sudden appearance, peering into the front passenger window made me jump. I glared at him as he tried the handle then opened it and slipped in beside me.

"I thought I saw you heading back here," he said as if the our last conversation hadn't ended with me ranting at him.

"Been following me?"

"I *was* keeping a lookout for you. It's not like I could just call you. That reminds me; we must exchange numbers," he added, gently patting my hand as if we were old school friends bumping into one another in the street. His purposely-civil tone made me feel a little remorse at my behaviour. "No, I've been a little busy, though a little concerned for your welfare."

I had a sudden flashback to the traffic lights and near-accident.

As if reading my mind, he went on. "Do you walk in front of cars often, or was it a spontaneous decision?"

"You saw that?"

He nodded. "I saw you get rescued by Super Gran. I thought you needed time to cool down, so I had a wander about. *Have* you cooled down?"

"Not sure," I muttered. "I'm just... angry at Gemma. You got caught in the crossfire."

Silence fell. He was looking back at me like he was expecting me to say more.

"What?" I asked, feeling awkward.

"I thought you were about to say sorry."

I frowned. "I *regret* having a go at you like that. But I'm not sorry. You have to lay off the sexy talk."

"Sexy talk?" His surprised tone and expression knocked me off-guard, and I laughed. "There we go. I thought to myself, 'Jack, if you can get her smiling, all shall be well!'"

"Expect it's not all well, is it?"

"Oh, I wouldn't be too hasty," he went on. "Could you step out of the car, madam?" He sounded like a 1950s London bobby.

"Why?" I asked, eyes narrowed.

"Because we ain't done with this town." Now he was a cowboy.

"What are you up to?"

"You shall find out, young Frodo." He reached across and took the keys from my hand

"Hey," I said, trying to grab them back. "I'm not leaving the car until you tell me what's going on."

"You won't get the keys back until you get out the car," he parried. I could smell coffee on his breath, and now I was becoming thirsty, not to mention hungry.

I gave him a look, and got out the car, trying not to let him see me smile as he got out his side.

We stood facing each other, separated by the car.

"Now what?" I asked.

He came around to my side, pocketing the keys then taking my arm in his, before leading me out the car park. "And now you shall indulge in some good food and fine wine, my treat."

"But not a devilishly handsome Englishman?" I asked

He pretended to straighten a tie and slicked back his hair. Then adopting the voice of Austin Powers, said: "Oh, behave."

CHAPTER TWELVE

Despite never having been in Inverness before, Jack appeared to know where he was going. I found myself doing a weird, haltering jog just to keep up with him. Once or twice he became hesitant, stopping to have a quick scan of our surroundings, before striding on.

"For some reason I always thought this place was a village. Never realised it was this big," he admitted

"Awarded city status in eighteen years ago," I told him, as we came to a stop at a crossing.

"Aw, it's just a baby. No plans to dash across the road right now?"

"Not until the green man flashes me," I answered.

"The mucky bugger."

"So where is your inbuilt SatNav taking us?" My belly gurgled just as I'd finished speaking. I hoped he hadn't heard.

"I think your stomach knows."

Damn, he *had* heard.

"There's your flasher," he added, as the traffic came to a stop and the green man appeared. Jack grabbed my hand. "Come on. Good food and fine wine awaits."

We reached the other side and walked past an art gallery, Starbucks, and a jewellers.

"An engagement ring? But, Jack, it's all so sudden!"

He smiled as he clocked the window full of ridiculously-expensive wedding and engagement rings as we passed.

"That's a bit presumptuous, Missy. What about you getting me a ring?"

I leant down and picked up a discarded ring-pull from some long-gone can and presented it to him.

He grimaced. "A dog might have peed on that."

"Eugh," I remarked, before dropping it again.

As Jack, still holding my hand, led me further along the road, his phone's ringtone started playing a tune I vaguely recognised from the 1990s

"At last," he said, coming to a stop and dropping my hand as he retrieved the buzzing object from his inside jacket pocket. "Alistair! Good news, I hope?"

I stood gazing at the surrounding architecture, failing not to listen to the one-sided conversation going on mere feet away.

"Good man!" Jack said, then gave me a thumbs-up sign. "And was it exactly what I asked for?" He listened while Alistair talked. "Excellent!" Another listen. "Oh, definitely," he said, turning to face me, his eyes giving me the once-over.

"How is Alistair, these days?" I asked, once the two men had said their goodbyes in the form of mild insults.

"He's doing very well. I'll tell him you were asking after him."

"Please do."

He grinned. "Okay, so it looks like we need to do a little detour before dinner." He checked his watch. "Just under an hour. I'd planned to have drinks first, but that can wait," he muttered, more to himself than to me.

"Detour to where?"

"To wherever you think you can find a decent present for Pete. I'm sure I saw a large shopping mall around here."

I remembered the sixty pounds languishing in my bank account. I couldn't get anything expensive. Certainly nothing the missing two hundred pounds could have bought.

"Sounds good," I told him, almost believing the enthusiasm I'd conjured up.

We reached the shopping mall, checking out store after store. Time was pressing on and nothing had inspired me.

We ended in a science fiction and fantasy memorabilia store. Pete and I had originally bonded over a love of creaky British science fiction shows. Being a self-confessed scifi nerd, this was the ideal place to find a gift for him.

While browsing the shelves of figurines, I discovered Jack flicking through a graphic novel. I glanced at the front cover, then looked at him. "You're a Whovian?"

He looked up from the booklet. "Born and bred. Why? Is that a deal-breaker?"

I shrugged, and continued my search. He didn't need to know I was a fan, too. He'd only say it was destiny we met. Probably with a Tom Baker impression.

"What are you grinning at?"

I jumped as he appeared next to me. "Nothing at all. Not seen anything you fancy?" I regretted asking as he smirked and raised an eyebrow.

"Apart from yours truly, seen anything *you* fancy? For Pete, I mean."

"A couple of things." Ones out of my price range, anyway.

On the far side of the shop a Sales sign had caught my eye. Below it were shelves of discounted goods. Maybe I'd have better luck, there. But when I went to move, I felt Jack gently take my arm.

"Don't worry about the price," he said in a quiet voice. "How much money had you collected?"

"About two hundred pounds, I think. What do you mean, 'don't worry about the price'?"

"I'll pay for his present. You can get anything up to £250, let's say."

I gawped at him. "I can't let you do that."

"Why not?"

"Because."

"Because? Heck, Carla, you'd make one hell of a lawyer. Why should your client get off scot-free? *Because*."

"You don't even know Pete."

"Old guy. Works as an editor. Ex-BBC employee. Yup, I know him."

"You know what I mean."

"Think of it as one friend helping out another. You had the money, but now you don't. I'm just lending you enough to cover it."

"Obviously it would be a loan, but -" I began.

"Excellent. I'll take that as an acceptance. Besides, I'd just badger you until you agreed."

"It's won't leave you out of pocket? That's a lot of money you're offering."

"I asked Alistair to put it on the company card for me."

Highland Fling didn't do company cards.

"You mean you have a card from your old job?" I asked.

"That's exactly what it is."

"And they haven't - I don't know - cancelled the card since you left?"

"It's a period of grace since I got the heartthrob gig fairly quickly."

"And the grace period includes adding money to the card?" It didn't make sense. Either he was fibbing, or his former employers were very generous.

"Have a good look round, take your time. Our table is booked for half four, though."

I checked the plain white wall clock above the counter where the bearded sales assistant, in a Nirvana T-shirt, was on the phone. "Crap we've only got fifteen minutes!"

"I know. So will you shut up and accept my very generous offer?" Jack asked.

I didn't have long to decide. "Okay, but never offer again."

"I'll try not to."

"Special circumstances, and all that," I told him, my eyes scanning the store for something. *Anything.*

"Of course."

"And I will pay you back, starting next payday." I led him across the floor towards a display window.

"Sure. But, you know, no rush."

We stopped in front of an almost life-size figure of a Dalek, surrounded by a ruffled black silk backdrop. I'd clocked it as soon as we'd entered the shop. Pete was a lifelong fan. His most treasured possessions being genuine autographs of every actor who had played the Doctor.

"Good choice," said Jack, taking in the size of the object.

"Can I help you?" The salesman, catching the whiff of a potential sale, had approached us.

"How much for this bad boy?" asked Jack, nodding up at the imposing figure.

"There's a discount for members. Either of you got a loyalty card?"

I shook my head. Jack did likewise.

"Ah. In that case, he's going to set you back £311.99."

That was way beyond Jack's budget. I could have added my sixty pounds, but I would have been left with nothing. "It doesn't matter," I told Jack. "I can get something else."

The sales guy looked at me. "A fan, eh? My girlfriend is mad for it, too. She only got into it 'cos of Tennant, but she likes some of the classic stuff, too. She's got a thing for a young Tom Baker, but she's always liked mad bastards." He laughed.

"Don't suppose we could get a discount, anyway?" asked Jack, chancing his luck. "It's a birthday present."

"Happy birthday." the guy said, looking at me before turning to Jack. "Sorry, pal. I don't make the rules."

"Okay, so what if I signed up for a loyalty card? Could I still get the discount?"

The man nodded. "That would work. If you'll just follow me." He led us back to the counter where he asked Jack several questions, got him to sign a form and then handed him a brand new loyalty card.

We reached the restaurant with a minute to spare.

CHAPTER THIRTEEN

We got our breath back once seated at our table; an intimate little booth in the corner of the quiet restaurant. A tea-light sat at the bottom of a long, thin glass container which cast a cosy glow.

The head waiter made sure we were both seated before producing two menus and setting them down before us. He took our drinks order then left us to choose our meals.

"Sure you don't want a small glass of wine?" Jack asked, viewing me over the menu in his hands.

"I'm driving, remember?"

He shrugged then focussed on choosing a starter.

"Thank you, by the way," I went on.

"Don't thank me yet. We haven't tasted the food."

"I didn't mean that. I meant Pete's present. You didn't need to."

"I wanted to." He smiled, then cast a look at the menu again. "Shall we share a starter?"

Our drinks arrived and the waiter departed with our food orders.

"Ah," said Jack, after taking a long sip of his ale. "That hits the spot."

"Jack."

He leant in. "Carla," he replied, the glow of the candle reflecting in his eyes.

"You didn't do all this to get into my good books, did you?"

"Are you asking if I'm trying to buy your affections?"

"I wouldn't put it quite so bluntly, but are you?"

He regarded me for a moment, then smiled fondly. "No. I know certain people think I'm a sex-mad creep, but I'm not trying to buy your affections. You definitely couldn't be bought. Even with a massive Dalek."

"I never called you a creep." I reached for my orange juice to hide my awkwardness. Those eyes... "Sex-mad but not a creep."

"You little charmer, you. And I wouldn't say I'm sex-mad, either."

"Maybe that was an exaggeration," I admitted. "But you like to flirt. A lot."

"That may be, but there's only one person I'm flirting with, if you hadn't noticed."

I couldn't hold his gaze. I looked down at the desserts section of the menu. "I'm not sure if I'm having pudding."

"Carla, look at me." His voice was gentle but firm. "If my flirting embarrasses you, then I'll stop."

The thing was, I *didn't* want him to stop. I loved the flirting. The attention he paid me. But always at the back of my mind, despite what she had done, was Gemma.

"Gemma likes you," I blurted out.

He looked puzzled. "I kind of gathered that from how she acts around me. But I don't know what she has to do with us."

Us. Was there an *us*? Sure we'd slept together, but that was a one-off.

Jack leant forward again. "I'll make this brief because you've turned the colour of a Royal Mail post box; it's quite endearing, actually. I like you a lot, Carla. I liked you a lot when we first met in that pub, and I like you just as much - though possibly just that little bit more since you've not teased me about my geeky preferences. I love being with you. I love your crazy ways and if you'll allow me a flashback, I love like kissing you. If you like me too - as much as I like you then please feel free to crawl across this table and ravage me. I realise what I've just said isn't particularly romantic, but then I'm not in a Richard Curtis movie." He finished, his own face tinged with pink.

What the hell kind of response could I give to that?

"I like Doctor Who, too," I told him.

"Marry me," he joked. "Anyway, enough of your incessant romantic gestures, Missy. I'm only here for the good food and fine wine - or rather, ale." He raised his glass in a toast.

"We'll forget about the devilishly handsome Englishman then, eh?" I said, relieved the awkwardness was over.

"Oh, I always indulge," he said, bringing the glass to his lips, then added. "Don't you?"

I stayed silent. Okay, so he'd laid his cards on the table as far as *we* were concerned. But part of me had a weird notion I was stealing Gemma's man. I know; ridiculous.

Talk turned to less personal matters: how Jack was getting on in his role as a Highland Heartthrob. I'd seen bits of footage Pete had edited together for the client's DVD. The accent had improved, but not enough to fool everyone. His first client had a tendency to chat him up. Proving his worth, and showing his commitment to the role, Jack stayed in character and always brought the conversation back within the confines of the time travel romance storyline.

"You're doing well," I told him. "Not all the guys would do that." Lance sprung to mind.

"It's a struggle," he admitted.

"She is pretty."

Jack laughed. "No, I don't mean that. Janice seems to forget what Highland Fling is all about." He rested his chin in his hand and sighed. "*A tawdry brothel but without the sex.*"

I recognised the quote. How could I not? It had been the parting shot in the hatchet-job from The Daily Informer.

I stared at him. "That bloody paper again. And you believed them, did you?"

"Well, I knew they were exaggerating, as usual. But I thought there must be some truth to it."

I dropped my fork with a clatter on the plate in front of me. "Truth? Christ, that paper wouldn't know truth if truth did a striptease in front of it and had the words I AM TRUTH tattooed on its chest."

"Interesting image."

"And the worst thing is, nobody bothered speaking to any of us. Somehow got hold of some photos from the old version of our website and wrote a ton of crap. I'd love to meet whoever wrote it.."

Jack was avoiding eye contact and taking a long sip of his drink. I guess I'd gone off on a rant again..

"I know you like the paper, but the business could have really been affected. They could have destroyed us."

"The owner of the paper found out his wife was a client," Jack said, meeting my eye. "He ordered the article to be written."

I frowned. "How do you know?"

"I know a couple of people in the media," he said, and drained the rest of his ale.

I still frowned as I processed this new piece of information. "Which client?"

"I don't know. Her husband found out and wasn't happy," shrugged Jack.

"So instead of doing proper research about us, he gets a minion to write some rubbish?" Marketing and HR held a meeting shortly after the article had been published. Concerns were raised. The Daily Informer's readership took their printed word as gospel.

"Look, let's not talk about it anymore," said Jack. "It's in the past. Highland Fling is doing fine. Let's talk about me, and how fabulous I am." He flashed a grin.

I continued eating in silence. He had a point. Apart from the odd troll on social media, the damage had been minimal.

Our desserts arrived - a chocolate brownie sundae for him and a slice of fudge cake for me - and I pushed all thoughts of the paper to the back of my mind. This was a rare night out for me. Good food, fine wine - I'd topped up my glass once I'd finished the orange juice - and enjoyable company. Especially the company. While Jack regaled me with tales of his research into Scottish accents (Rab C. Nesbitt and Trainspotting), my mind was full of What Ifs:

What if Jack didn't work at *Highland Fling*? What if our one-night stand had become two, three, four? Was my rule against office romances compelling me to keep my distance? Was it really because Gemma liked him too?

"Earth to Carla." Jack waved his spoon in front of my face.

"Sorry, what were you saying?"

"I was droning on, wasn't I?" he asked. "Sorry."

"No, not at all. I was just... thinking."

"Anything interesting?"

"I want to go dancing," I said, surprising myself.

"You've heard about my legendary moves?"

"No, I was thinking of *my* legendary moves." I winked..

"Are there any clubs around here?" He asked, and started eating his dessert with more haste.

"There's got to be some."

It's not quite half six yet. There won't be any open yet."

I shrugged. "We can go for a drink somewhere first."

"You're driving, remember?"

Another shrug. "I've already had a glass of your wine. We'll just have to find a hotel afterwards," I said, and avoided his gaze. "Twin beds, of course," I added, as an afterthought.

CHAPTER FOURTEEN

We entered *Spades* nightclub just gone 9pm. The club was old-school, complete with glitterball, and just off the city centre where commercial buildings gave way to residential areas. I'd booked us into the last twin room in a nearby hotel.. We'd both showered - *separately*, I may add - to freshen up before hitting the town in search of a club that was thirty-something friendly.

I knew *Spades* was my kind of place when I heard the music; Pet Shop Boys which led into Blondie by the time we reached the bar. The dance floor was jumping with a crowd of dancers of all ages.

"What would you like to drink?" asked Jack, bringing out his wallet. I shook my head and made a face.

"Nothing yet. I just want to dance," I said, my hips swaying to the beat.

He smiled and returned the wallet to his coat pocket. "Your wish is my command. Come on, missy. Show me your moves."

The next couple of hours flew by so quickly I hardly noticed. Much of it spent dancing with Jack. We sat out the slow songs, though he tried to keep me on the dance floor once or twice.

We perched on bar stools, sipping our drinks while 10CC insisted they weren't in love. I peered at Jack's watch.

"Bloody hell! Almost midnight already!" I leant across and spoke into his ear.

"Are you going to turn into a pumpkin soon?" Jack asked, playfully.

"Maybe," I said, playing with the straw of my cocktail. "Best get back to the hotel. I forgot to ask if they have a curfew."

"Curfew?" Jack asked, once we'd left the club. The cool air instantly hit us so we stood for a minute, waiting for the effect to wear off.

I nodded. "The first time I came up to north of Scotland my friend and I were told that if we weren't there by ten-thirty, the front door would be locked and we'd have to find a nice bench to sleep on for the night."

"Charming."

"I think we'll be okay here, though. It was a long time ago, and the couple who ran the B&B had very conservative views"

"I'm guessing your *friend* was of the male persuasion?"

I nodded. "You guess right."

When we finally reached the hotel and got to our room, Jack switched the television on while I filled the kettle from the tap in the adjoining bathroom.

"*Hot Fuzz* again? I'm sure that movie was just on the other day," I remarked, watching as Simon Pegg made a dry comment to Nick Frost on-screen.

"Probably," agreed Jack, settling down on one of the beds. "Good film, though."

I took off my shoes, glad to be free of them, and watched the film until the kettle turned itself off. .

"Relax. I'll do these,' he said, tearing a sachet open with his teeth before dropping the tea bag inside into a cup.

I wasn't going to argue. I sat on the bed he'd just vacated, and rested my back against the wall with my legs stretched out before me. I was conscious of Jack stealing glances at me through the mirror as I continued viewing the film.

"What is it?" I asked, checking my hair for any sticky-up bits..

"You're sexy when you dance."

"Shut up," I said, embarrassed.

"You are. You seemed to be in another world on the dance floor. I wasn't the only admirer tonight."

"Shut up," I repeated, smiling this time.

"Just telling the truth," Jack said with a shrug. He brought across the drinks and motioned for me to make space for him.

"And what's wrong with that one?" I asked, nodding towards the empty single bed a foot away.

"It hasn't got sexy people on it."

"I'll ban you from saying the word 'sexy'," I said, taking a cautious sip of tea.

"Oh yes? And what will happen if I defy your ban?"

I thought about this for a moment, trying not to think of anything that would bring out Mr Innuendo again. "I'd find out all your secrets and blackmail you with them. God, you'd love that, wouldn't you?" I added, seeing the inspired smile spreading across his face.

He nodded. "You can blackmail me anytime."

"Geez, you can make *any* word sound rude," I said, laughing.

"It's a gift."

We focussed on the film, speaking only to remark upon the action on the screen. When the credits appeared, I yawned and stretched my arms. Jack was in the bathroom, rinsing the cups.

"Tired?" He asked, coming back into the main room and sitting the cups down next to the kettle.

I nodded. "It's been a long day."

"Buying Daleks will do that to a person," said Jack.

"*You* bought the thing, not me," I reminded him. "Thank you. It was really generous of you. But I will pay -" I paused as he grimaced and held up a hand in protest.

"There's no rush. Anyway, you paid for the room so you can call that as part-repayment." He sat down on the other bed.

"No, I want to pay you back the full amount."

"I'll ban you from saying the phrase 'pay you back.'"

I smiled. "And what if I defy the ban?"

"Well, there's only one punishment I can really dish out."

"And what's that?"

"I'd have to kiss you. And I mean a deep, leaves-you-speechless, devastating kiss." His eyes twinkled.

"I'd better behave then," I told him.

"Oh you really don't have to, on my account."

"I'm going to sleep," I said, catching him off-guard..

"I think I'll get my head down, too. Thank you for the enjoyable and unpredictable day, Carla Kingston." He nodded his head in acknowledgement.

"My pleasure, Jack Jefferson." I slipped under the purple bedding, fully clothed, and intentionally faced away from him.

"Sweet dreams," I heard him whisper. Seconds later, the lights went out.

Lying there with eyes shut, I was aware of everything: the subdued traffic outside; the sound of late-night revellers passing in the street below; that Jack lay mere feet away from me. I hoped I wouldn't snore.

I wondered if I'd snored last time.

I listened out for any audible sign of him sleeping. Apart from a slight creak coming from his bed, I couldn't tell.

Just worry about you *getting some sleep*, I admonished myself. Try as I did, it was not forthcoming. I had too much on my mind: my upcoming holiday; Gemma and Lance. I was tempted to check my phone for any missed calls from her, but the light from the screen might wake Jack.

If he was asleep.

"Pay," I whispered.

Nothing.

"Pay you."

Not a peep. Maybe he *was* asleep.

"Pay you back," I finished and then prepared to drift of to slumberland.

Not a minute had passed when a voice spoke in the darkness.

"You were warned."

I froze. "I thought you were asleep."

"Nope. Just lying here wondering the same thing about you. Until you broke the ban."

"I don't think the ban was put in place," I countered.

"It was. A full minute before you broke it."

"Bad timing," I said into the darkness.

"For you, perhaps."

I'm glad he couldn't see me smiling.

I waited. There was no movement coming from the other bed. Instead, I felt a surprising pang of disappointment he wasn't carrying through with the 'threat'.

"Hello."

Startled at the voice in my ear, I nearly fell out of the other side of the bed, grabbing onto the side just in time.

Light flooded the room as Jack switched on the main light switch. "You okay?" He asked, managing to look both concerned and sheepish at the same time.

"I am now, Ninja Nigel," I said, getting my breath back as I sat up. "I never heard you move!"

"I was trying my best to sneak up on you."

"You certainly did that. I was expecting a kiss, not be frightened to death."

"Sorry." He bowed his head for a moment in embarrassment, then looked up with a grin. "You were *expecting* a kiss, eh?"

"I *was*." I pulled the bed sheets up from where they'd made a bid for freedom.

Jack moved into the gap between the two beds and sat down on the edge of mine. "I *am* sorry. It was a silly thing to do."

"Yes, it was."

He nodded. "I think I should just kiss you now. It's been hyped up enough. If I don't then, I'll dream about it and wake up snogging my pillow."

"You're right. It's best to get it over and done with." I sat up straight, closed my eyes and pursed my lips.

"You look like you're ready to take a selfie," I heard him say.

"You're running out of time," I said, speaking through the tight pout, eyes still shut.

"Oh." I heard him shift and felt him nearing me.

I giggled.

"Well, I don't usually get that response until at least *after* I've kissed someone."

I gave him a sheepish look. "Sorry."

"You seem nervous. You do remember that we've spent the night together before?. I've seen every lovely inch of you. Nothing to be nervous about."

"Sorry."

"Don't apologise. It's kind of cute you've gone all shy."

I cleared my throat. "Right, I'm good. Snog away." I closed my eyes again, more out of embarrassment than anything else.

"Look at me." His voice was soft.

I did. He was shaking his head with a smile on his face.

"You're some woman," he declared.

While I was trying to come up with a witty, sexy response he cupped the side of my face with a warm hand and stroked my cheek with his thumb. Then he pulled me gently towards him.

CHAPTER FIFTEEN

I woke around 7am clinging onto the edge of the single bed that wasn't made for two grown adults. Jack's arm rested across my shoulder and his warm breath hit the back of my neck. My joints were stiff and I could do with getting more comfortable, but didn't want to wake him. Besides, if I tried to shift, there was a good chance one or both of us would fall out of the bed. I lay there until the urge to move overcame me. Slowly I stretched my legs and twisted until I was on my back.

"Not planning on doing a runner again, are you?" He sounded drowsy.

"No. Not today."

"Good." He shifted onto his side. "Well, this is refreshing. Waking up to find you still here."

"Hey, I could leave if it's too weird," I offered.

"It's the good kind of refreshing."

"Is there a bad kind?"

"A philosophical conundrum for a Sunday morning. I think it could be discussed over breakfast. Hungry?"

My belly chose that very moment to respond.

Jack laughed. "I guess you are."

We dressed them then went for breakfast. Well, I got dressed. Jack found a tartan dressing robe someone had left in the wardrobe. Thankfully he wore his boxer shorts underneath.

Afterwards, we returned to our room to pick up our things and checked out. On our way back to the car, we passed the shop where the Dalek remained on display.

"Does Pete have room for that big boy?" Jack asked. He'd been fidgeting with his phone since we'd left the hotel, but it was now back in his pocket.

"His house is bigger on the inside," I joked. "His spare room is practically a shrine to science fiction shows. He'll make space for it."

"And how are we getting it from my place to his?"

"Magic." I felt Jack take my hand in his.

"So, I was thinking," he began, "Once we get back, what would you say to staying at mine for dinner?"

"You can cook?"

"See for yourself."

"Tempting, but I need to get my stuff ready for Wednesday. It's the only time I have to do it."

"Wednesday?"

"My holiday, remember? I'm sure I told you."

"It rings a bell. How long will you be away for?"

"Just a week."

"Hmm."

"Hmm?"

"Sorry, I was just deciding if it would be too cheesy to say I'll miss you," Jack confessed, giving my hand a squeeze.

"It's kind of sweet, actually."

"Good. And I hope it's not too cheesy to add that I'll pray nightly that you don't meet a bronzed adonis in - where is it you're going?"

"Spain."

"Bronzed adonis in Spain."

"You're going to have to pray *really* hard," I told him.

We returned to Auchtermachen an hour later. I dropped Jack off first - and received a kiss that almost made me change my mind about the dinner offer - before returning home.

I hate Sundays. Too quiet, even more so in a tiny village. If I didn't have the internet or a television, I think I'd go mad. There's only so many times you can go for walks. And that's if the weather is decent.

After having a quick lunch while watching a repeat of an old british sitcom, I went to pack for the holiday. The list of things I needed lay on my bedside table. As the navy blue suitcase was filled, I ticked off each item until all that was left was sunscreen. A quick trip to the supermarket was in order.

Twenty minutes later, I searching the aisles. Being November, there wasn't much call for summer accessories, but amongst the body lotions and shower creams, I found one bottle of sunscreen.

"Well, well. Fancy seeing you here," said a familiar voice that made me look up.

Jack stood before me, basket in hand. I clocked a pint of milk, a packet of porridge and bag of sugar.

"Going native?" I asked with a nod towards the groceries.

"Apparently I used to eat porridge as a child. Thought I'd give it a try again." He noticed the lotion in my hand. "Got everything packed?"

"Almost."

"You know that offer still stands. I'm happy to forgo my porridge-eating nostalgia trip and make you dinner. I'm willing to make that sacrifice."

I thought back to my kitchen, and the half dozen ready meals in the freezer. "I tell you what, get the ingredients you need, we'll split the cost, and you can cook at mine."

He seemed surprised at my change of heart. "You can't resist me, huh?"

"I'm intrigued to know how good - or bad - a cook you are. What were you planning on cooking, by the way?"

"You'll just have to wait and see. And I'll pay for the ingredients. I needed to buy them, anyway."

"Do you want me to provide the dessert?"

A wicked grin spread across his face. Yeah, okay. So the question wasn't entirely innocent. But then, he hasn't got first dibs on the ol' innuendo.

"I'll take that as a yes," I said, brushing past him towards the dessert aisle.

"Oh, you're in trouble, Missy," I heard him say after me.

I looked at him, over my shoulder. "Good."

Once home, I directed him towards the kitchen while I raced to the living room and took all the underwear down from the clotheshorse in the corner. Chances were, if he'd clocked those, it would end up a very late dinner. Throwing the bras and knickers onto my bed, I returned to find Jack kneeling in front of the open freezer door.

"Pass me the gateau, please."

"There you go."

"Do you always have ready meals?" he asked, sliding the box into a drawer.

"I can't be bothered cooking for one," I admitted.

"We can't have that. I'll be expecting a feast next time I'm here. At least five courses."

"So that'll be beans on toast, mince and tatties, pizza, a pasta bake and a baked potato, then."

He stared at me. "Is that genuinely all you can cook?"

I shrugged. "Nobody showed me when I was younger. At college it was always ready meals or eating out." I frowned. "I hope you're not implying that just because I'm female I should know how to cook," I said, only half-teasing.

"Not at all. I think everyone should know how to cook."

"Well, I know how to cook at least five things, so I'm not a total hopeless case."

"Never said you were. And I'm quite intrigued by the mince and tatties. That's minced beef and potatoes, isn't it?"

I nodded. "Yup. Scotland's unofficial dish."

"I look forward to tasting it next Sunday."

"Next Sunday? I'll still be in Spain."

He adopted a puppy-dog expression. "Aw, you had to mention the S-word."

"There is always the Sunday after that, though."

He smiled. "I'll mark it in my diary."

"It's a bit early for dinner. Why don't you sit down? I think I've got biscuits in the cupboard."

We ended up in the Snug, a small room off the kitchen where I'd set up a comfy sofa and a shelving unit which housed a small TV, an even smaller music system, and enough books to fill a mobile library.

"This is nice and *snug*," Jack said, as he sat down on the teal two-seater sofa. I put the biscuit barrel down on the upturned crate that served as a table and joined him.

"I use it more than the living room, if I'm honest. Closer to the kettle and fridge."

"Bit of a bookworm, eh?" He asked as his eyes scanned the rows of books. "Is that Harry Potter I spot?"

"One of them. I've got all seven."

"But they're not together."

"I got bored one night last week and arranged them in alphabetical order. Don't judge me."

"Wasn't planning to. I have mine arranged by spine colour."

"I can't remember seeing a bookshelf at your place," I said.

"You were too focussed on yours truly to bother about books," Jack replied, his arm finding its way across my shoulders.

"I bet you've never cracked open a book in your life," I teased, settling against him.

"Oh really? I'll have my well-thumbed book back, then."

"What well-thumbed book?"

"The one I left in the pub the night we met."

I had to think for a moment. The only book I remember is the one by Robert Harris. *This book is yours to finish. Please leave it somewhere so someone else can take pleasure in it*, someone had scribbled on the title page.

"*You* left that book?"

He nodded. "Guilty as charged. I'd heard about Bookcrossing before - you know, where one person leaves a book in a public place -"

"-someone picks it up, reads it, and does the same thing," I finished for him.

"Something like that, yeah. I'd finished that one and thought I'd leave it up in the Highlands for a Scot to peruse."

"You have good taste."

"Obviously," he laughed.

"In books, I meant." I nudged him in the chest with my elbow.

"So did I."

CHAPTER SIXTEEN

I headed to work the next morning, mentally prepared to face Gemma. Whether she was ready to face me was another matter. I stopped at the reception desk where Pierre sat, immaculately-dressed as always, with a smile for me.

"Good morning, Carla. Did you have a good weekend?" He asked, in that gorgeous accent of his.

"It was.. interesting," I replied, with a smile.

He raised an eyebrow. "Oh? Tell me more."

"Maybe later. Has Gemma arrived yet?" I normally had time to chat but today I had other things on my mind.

"Ah, non. I haven't seen her."

I nodded. "Okay. Could you tell her to come and see me when she gets in, please?"

"Oui. Is everything alright?"

"Everything's fine," I said, brightly.

Once I reached my office, I woke the computer and grabbed a cup of tea before going through the pile of mail on my desk.

Every couple of minutes I'd check my Lync contacts on screen, but Gemma was still marked as *Offline*. She couldn't hide from me forever.

When there came a tap on the door fifteen minutes later, I'd been so engrossed in a new report into tourism in the Highlands that I'd almost forgotten about Gemma. Flustered, I closed the tab on the computer and turned to face the door.

"Come in." My voice was sharp, devoid of warmth. I wanted her to walk in the room looking ashamed.

But it was Pete, looking anything but ashamed. He was laughing. Too cheery for a Monday morning, I decided.

"You feeling okay?" I asked.

"Yeah, yeah. I'm fine."

I watched him through narrowed eyes as he sat himself down in the chair opposite me. "Good weekend?"

He shrugged. "Not bad."

"Do you know if Gemma's in yet?" I asked, checking my screen again.

"No idea."

"If you see her, tell her to come and see me as soon as she can."

Pete watched me. "What's happened? I can tell that look on your face. What's she done now?"

I dismissed the issue. I wasn't about to tell him about the stolen birthday money.

"Actually," Pete continued. "I was going to call you yesterday. We were thinking -"

"We?" I grinned, assuming he was speaking about Hazel.

The door swept open again. Here she was finally, jacket still on and handbag slung over one shoulder.

"You in a better mood yet?" she asked briskly.

I made a noise that sounded like "Pfft."

"Thought so." She glanced at Pete then left.

"Oh, hang on, lady!" I shouted, leaping up from my chair and following her out. I nearly knocked Pete off his chair on my quest to catch Gemma. "Sorry," I apologised, rushing into the corridor. Gemma was making for the lifts.

"Gemma, stop!"

She came to a stop. Her body rose and fell with a heavy sigh. As she faced me, it felt like high noon in an old western.

"What do you want, Carla?" She said, hand on hip.

"I want you to tell me you found him and have got the money." I bit back.

"No, I didn't find him. But here -" She opened her bag and lobbed a well-sealed envelope at me. I caught it before it hit the floor. "Here's your bloody money. Are we done?"

"It's all here?"

"Count it. I've got work to do." She turned heel and disappeared into the lift. I would have gone after her but my desk phone was ringing. I'd catch up with her later. At least I'd got the money back.

I saw no one else the entire morning. At lunchtime, I took a trip to the cafeteria, hoping I'd Gemma would be there. Since she'd returned all the money (yes, I'd counted it), I wanted to know if she'd caught up with Lance, or if she'd managed to gather it herself

There was no sign of her when I got my lunch, but I sat at a table, anyway. I'd swing by the makeup department on my way back to my desk.

Pete was in the queue with his usual sandwich and ginger beer. I waved at him and nodded towards the empty chair opposite me. He pointed across to where Hazel was cautiously sipping the soup of the day.

I gave him the thumbs-up, then made a love heart sign with my fingers. I laughed when he scowled and stuck up his middle finger. I was glad he and Hazel were getting on so well. They were well-suited. And if it meant an end to Gemma's insinuations about him and I, then who was I to stand in the way?

Reminded of the makeup artist, I kept an eye on the cafeteria door as people came and went. Still no sign of Gemma, though.

Now I was starting to feel bad. Yes, what she did was a shitty thing, but I had the money again. And she'd gone all the way to Glasgow to find Lance in the first place. I didn't want to go on holiday without sorting things out.

I finished my lunch quickly then headed to the dressing room. While the Heartthrobs were busy filming, the costume artists got to work, making sure outfits were in pristine condition.

Except Gemma wasn't there. According to her colleagues, she'd gone up to the editing suite to watch the morning's rushes.

I tapped on the door, out of habit, then walked in. Gemma was sitting on Pete's usual chair, headphones clamped to her ears, watching footage of Jack and his client. She hadn't noticed I was there. Or if she knew, then she was ignoring me. I spoke her name. No answer. Tried again.

This time she took the earphones off her head and spun round on the chair. "I wasn't listening to anything. I don't know how to adjust the volume on this bloody thing," she muttered, putting the earphones down on the desk with a clatter.

"We need to talk," I said, taking the empty chair next to her.

She folded her arms. "You did plenty of that on Saturday."

"I was angry. You would be, too."

"Oh, I was. Raging. Probably the most dangerous person in Glasgow over the weekend, searching for that prick. Came up with many creative scenarios for when I eventually caught up with him, too"

"Did you?"

"No," she admitted. "But one day when he least expects it. When he's busy trying to con another - what did you call me - ah yes, another 'sad, desperate old woman.' I'll be ready."

"I don't think I called you old," I said, risking a joke to diffuse the tension.

It worked. The corners of her mouth curved slightly. "No, just sad and desperate."

"No, you're not," I protested.

"Yes, I bloody am. At least I can see that. I suppose Lance has done me a favour, in a way."

"What do you mean?"

"I know how I act sometimes, Carla. Around men."

"You just... like flirting. Nothing wrong with that," I countered.

"There is when you're making a fool of yourself. I never thought there'd ever be a time where I stole money for some guy."

"Yeah, it was a stupid thing to do -," I began.

"Thanks." She muttered.

"- but you did it with the understanding he'd give you back the money straightaway, not do a runner."

"You haven't told anyone else what happened, have you?" Gemma asked. "I mean, it's theft. A sackable offence. I can't afford to be out of work."

"No one else knows. Just you, me and Lance." There was no need to mention Jack. He wouldn't breathe a word.

"We can look for something for Pete tonight after work?" Gemma offered. "We can take my car."

I hesitated. "I got him something. Scraped some enough money together."

"What did you get?"

I grinned. "All in good time."

"So," Gemma said, standing up. "Forgive and forget?"

"Forgive over time, but I can forget now." I thought she was about to go for a hug. Instead she squeezed my shoulder and moved towards the door. "Oh, and I'm taking your advice," she added.

"What advice?"

"I'm going to try and make a go of it with Jack. Properly, this time. No messing about."

"Great," I said in a small voice.

CHAPTER SEVENTEEN

I didn't see the object of Gemma's affections that day due to filming commitments. A couple of texts came through when I was getting ready for bed, later that night. I confess to hearing his voice when reading them. Soppy, I know!

I lay there with the intention of falling asleep, but my mind seemed most active at night. Instead of sleep, I thought about what Gemma had said.

I should have told her, there and then, about Jack and I. Stopped her from doing anything embarrassing. So why hadn't I? Was it revenge for what she'd done? I didn't think I was that heartless.

I didn't know for certain where I stood with Jack. Were we dating? An item? Or just two people who'd slept together a couple of times?

I met him for lunch the next day. He was on his two-day break so was more than happy to meet me.

"Our little boy is coming home today," he said, over a coffee and panini. "I got a text from that scifi shop. It should be here around four."

"Good. I'm glad it'll be here before I leave tomorrow. Do you think it'll fit in my car?"

"If you push the back seat down, it might."

"Right, I'll swing by yours after work. I brought my car with me today."

He grinned. "Any excuse to see me, eh?"

"I only want you for your Dalek," I confessed with a straight face.

"Ah, but you still want me."

I wasn't the only one. I needed to tell him - warn him? - about Gemma. I'd be gone for a week. Who knows what she might try in the meantime.

"I'll make us something," he added. "What do you fancy?"

"Anything," I replied, still musing over Gemma.

"So roasted, broken glass with a side dish of used nappy and a serving of cat pee sauce?"

I looked at him. "What?"

"You okay today? You seem distracted. Not having second thoughts?"

"Second thoughts?" I asked, blowing on the hot chocolate in front of me.

"About us."

I watched him over the rim of my cup as I took a sip.

"Ah. Silence isn't good." His default grin faltered.

"I wasn't thinking about that, but since you've broached the subject."

"Uh-oh."

"I just want to know... I don't know..." I tried to speak, but this was bloody awkward. I felt like a little girl asking a boy if he liked her. "When I'm in Spain and *if* I get chatted up -" He made a face at this. I could feel my face burn, but I carried on. "Do I tell them I have a boyfriend back home, or...?"

"I'd appreciate it."

"Oh."

"Oh?"

"I wasn't sure where we stood. If this is just a casual thing or - not that the alternative is marriage!" I added with a smile.

"I know what you're meaning. Well, I can't speak for you, but I like how things are going. Aren't you?"

I nodded. "I am."

"Glad to hear it. If it puts your mind at rest, I see you as my hot Scottish girlfriend, or me as your disgustingly handsome boyfriend, if you'd prefer."

My face was still flushed. Now the awkwardness was out of the way, I needed to tell him about Gemma. It wasn't fair on her, or him.

Before I speak, he reminded me of the time. I had ten minutes to get back to work. I'd tell him later when we moved Pete's gift.

Five o'clock on the dot, I was already out of my office and heading outside. I'd sent Jack a text to say I'd be five minutes, and to get the kettle on. Winter had arrived early; the village was awash with snow.

I got as far as my car before I heard my name being called. Gemma was rushing my way, wrapping a purple cashmere scarf around her neck; her coat only zipped halfway up.

"Good, I caught you," she said, reaching me. "Fancy giving me a lift?"

I mentally worked out where Gemma lived, where Jack's cottage was, and figured I could drop her off, turn the car around and drive back.

"Sure."

I stuck the windscreen wipers on as the flurry from before was now a small blizzard. Gemma got in beside me and shoved three shopping bags down by her feet.

"Looking forward to Spain?" She asked, as we pulled away from the car park.

"It can't come quick enough."

Gemma told me about the holiday she was taking next summer; already she'd used up her holiday allowance for this year.

"Hawaii?"

"My aunt lives in Molokai," explained Gemma. "Hang on, is that someone standing in the middle of the road? What are they bloody doing? They're going to get themselves killed"

I peered through the windscreen. She was right. Through the blizzard, I could see someone stand on the far side of the road, waving at us.

"Maybe someone's broke down," I said.

"Can't see a car."

We came to a stop. The headlights lit up the figure wrapped in a warm jacket, scarf and red bobble hat.

"It's Jack!" Gemma cried with delight.

I frowned and looked again. The man approached my side of the car, and on closer inspection I realised she was right. He knocked on the car window and I reluctantly wound it down.

"Hey, se-" he began, but I interrupted him before he could say more.

"Jack! What are you doing out in weather like this?" I asked, before turning to Gemma who was giving him a warm, toothy smile.

"I know something that'll warm you -" Gemma started, before correcting herself. "Hi Jack," she finished, instead.

"Gemma, you two ladies made up then?"

I gave him a piercing stare. He wasn't supposed to know what had been going on.

"I told Jack we'd had a falling out," Gemma admitted.

"Oh really?" I asked, looking at Jack again. All this head-turning was making me dizzy.

"But it's all sorted now," Gemma went on.

"Glad to hear it. Anyway, Carla. I got your text message, so I thought I'd meet you outside the cottage." He continued, crouching down outside the car and leaning his arms on the window frame.

"Text message?" Gemma asked.

Think fast, Carla.

"The present I got Pete. It sent it to Jack's, by mistake," I said, hoping she'd take the bait.

"Typical," said Gemma. "That happens to me all the time."

"So I told Jack I'd come round and collect it after work," I went on.

"Ooh!" Gemma rubbed her hands together. "Can't wait to see it."

"It's inside," said Jack. "I didn't want to bring it out in this weather, until you arrived." He explained.

"Okay." I got out the car. "Stay there, Gemma. Won't be long."

"Fine by me," said Gemma, shivering at the cold air infiltrating the car.

Jack and I headed back to the cottage.

"Everything okay?" He asked, for the second time that day. "You seemed on edge, back there."

"Gemma doesn't know about us, yet," I told him, as I followed him into the hallway.

"Why not? Am I your dirty little secret?" He asked, with a smile.

"I haven't found the right time."

We entered the living room where the Dalek sat, the top of its casing poking out of a large wooden crate.

"I had to open it to check it was okay," explained Jack.

"That's alright. Oh, and I've got something for you back at mine."

"Really? Tell me more." He came across and wrapped his arms around my waist. If Gemma happened to walk in at that moment...

"She paid back the money," I said. "So I can pay you back for this big boy."

"She did? That's good. But no need to pay me back right away. I can get the money when you come back from Spain."

"Okay. Anyway, we'd better get Dalek Fred into the car, or Gemma will wonder what we're doing." I extracted myself from his embrace and took in the size of the collectable.

Jack had found a heavy duty trolley in the shed earlier so, together, we slid the Dalek-occupied crate onto it. Jack guided it outside while I made sure he didn't knock into anything.

"Bloody hell, I thought you'd bought him something that could fit in a plastic bag. What is that thing?" Gemma was leaning against the car, having a smoke but she threw the cigarette away and stood upright as the present was pushed towards her.

"It's a Dalek. From Doctor Who," I explained, as I opened the boot and started dismantling the back seat to make room.

"You got him *that*?" I caught the grimace on Gemma's face.

"I think it's a great present," said Jack.

"Don't worry," I told Gemma. "Pete will love it. Help us get it in here."

Gemma dropped her cigarette to the snow-covered ground and, between the three of us, and with several muttered swear words filling the air, we got the Dalek into the boot.

"Jesus, I'm never doing that again," said Gemma, getting her breath back.

"I didn't think it would fit," Jack admitted. "The boot must be bigger on the inside."

Gemma didn't share the joke. Instead, she moved so she was standing between Jack and I, facing him. "Actually, Jack. I was wondering if I could have a word."

Jack looked at me. I shrugged back, but inside I felt... odd. Was she wanting some privacy so she could ask him out?

"Yeah, I'll see you at work tomorrow, Gem," he said, pleasantly.

"I was sort of meaning now."

"I thought you and Carla were going somewhere."

"Nah, she was just giving me a lift. I can -" she paused and looked up at the deluge of snow now falling, "-walk home."

"In this?" I said, with slight incredulity. If it was a toss-up between walking and getting a lift, she would choose the former every time. Not to mention the fact, she lived a good twenty minute walk away, and that was on a non-snowy day.

"Why don't you both come in and I'll make us all a cuppa?" Jack suggested.

"Okay," I said, then saw a flash of annoyance cross Gemma's face.

"Great!" She said instead, linking arms with us both. "Let's get out of this bloody snow. I was beginning to lose the feeling in my feet, anyway."

Once we were all inside, Jack and I went through to the kitchen, while Gemma went to use the loo, reminding us that she'd already been to Jack's before.

In the kitchen, a pot of something delicious was bubbling away. Jack gave it a stir with a spoon and then filled the kettle up at the sink.

"Is that the meal you were making for tonight?" I asked, taking a seat at the table.

"It's the meal I *am* making for tonight." He corrected. "I guess you still haven't told her?"

"Haven't found the right time. Anyway, when exactly was she complaining to you about me, huh?" I asked, remembering what Gemma had said earlier.

"She called me this morning. Didn't realise I had another day off. Yeah, you were mentioned quite a bit."

"I bet I was."

"Anyway," he continued, coming around the table and wrapping his arms around me again. He smelt good. "It's over. No need to worry about it. I am all yours."

"You'd better not be doing this when she comes back," I warned him.

He sighed and let go of me, heading back to the counter to get three mugs from the cupboard. "I really don't know why you're hung up about her finding out. She will, sometime. The longer you leave it, the worse it will be."

"Yeah, I mean. We may as well do it right here on the kitchen table, so she can be under no illusion, huh?" I said sarcastically, then added quickly. "That was a joke. So keep any comments to yourself, please."

He laughed and finished preparing the drinks.

There was an awkwardness in the air as the three of us sat with our drinks, making idle conversation. I knew Gemma wished I wasn't there; I wished Gemma wasn't there, and Jack kept giving me significant looks whenever Gemma hinted about staying for that "lovely dinner you're making".

After we'd moved to the living room and were on our second cups, I decided now was as good a time as any. I wanted to enjoy my holiday, not spend it worrying about Gemma. Besides, with Jack being here, too, I would get less kickback.

Then again, maybe she would be okay. Wish us luck and be happy for us.

Hmm.

I took a deep breath. "Gemma, I've got something to tell you."

"Ooh, sounds ominous," she laughed, then her smile faded. "What is it, Caz? You're not ill, are you?"

"No, nothing like that."

"Are you-?" began Jack.

"Yes, yes," I said in a loud voice, drowning out the rest of his question.

Gemma laughed nervously. "You're starting to worry me. What is it?"

"Okay. Well, the thing is -"

Jack's landline took that moment to ring. Both Gemma and I looked at him.

"It'll be a wrong number again. Just ignore it," he said, staying where he was. "Carry on, Carla. You were saying?"

I waited until the call went to voicemail. "Right. So, what it is is-"

"Jack!" A gruff Australian voice barked from nowhere. "What the hell do you think you're playing at? Pick up the damn phone!"

The change on Jack's face was startling. He almost tripped over the coffee table in his haste to get to the phone.

"Tanya tells me you've not checked-in for about a week!" The man growled. "You know you're meant to -"

"Hi, hi. I'm here. Sorry." Jack said into the phone, having practically torn it from its stand.

Gemma and I exchanged looks and then did that thing where you pretend to be interested in something else, but really you're listening to the one-sided conversation.

"Yes, I'm sorry. A couple of things have come up," Jack was saying. He took the portable phone into the hallway, giving us an apologetic look as he did so. He closed the door after him, and we heard another door closer after that. Obviously it was a conversation he didn't want us to hear.

"Wonder who that was," Gemma said, helping herself to the last biscuit on the plate.

I shrugged. "Whoever it was sounded very cheesed off."

"Cheesed off? That's an understatement. I expected the guy to burst out the phone."

"I wonder if it's about the card," I began to say, remembering what Jack had said about still having his company card. Was the angry guy someone from his old workplace? Maybe he wasn't supposed to be using it after all.

"What card?" Gemma asked.

"Oh, it's nothing," I said.

The door opened. Jack swept in and placed the phone back on its charging dock. "Sorry about that," he said.

"Everything okay?" I asked.

"Yeah, who was that guy? Sounded like he was spitting feathers," said Gemma.

"It was just someone I know back in London. Doesn't matter. Anyway, you'd better get the Dalek back to Carla's before the snow gets any heavier."

"Oh, I wouldn't mind getting stuck here," said Gemma in a soft voice.

"Jack's right," I said, finishing my tea. I got to my feet. The smell of dinner was making my stomach growl. "We'd best get back."

I saw Gemma pout, but she reluctantly got up, anyway. "Hang on," she said. "What were you about to tell me before?"

"It can wait," I said, and heard a small exasperated sound escape Jack's lips.

It was only when we were putting our coats back on, that I realised that I would have to humph the Dalek into the house myself, once I'd dropped Gemma off.

"What are you doing?" Gemma asked Jack, who was slipping his coat on.

"Well, I'm not being sexist, but I doubt Carla will be able to carry the Dalek into her house by herself."

I smiled. He must have been reading my mind.

"But there's no room," Gemma went on. "You can't sit in the back with that *Dariek* there."

"Dalek," Jack and I said, in unison.

"She's right," I said to Jack. "There's no room."

"Not unless someone sits on someone's lap in the front," Gemma trilled, looking at Jack.

"Okay," I said, "here's what we'll do. I'll drop Gemma off, come back for Jack, and then we can take the Dalek home."

"But -" Gemma protested, but Jack agreed it was a good idea, and went to check on the dinner. "Thanks, Carla," she hissed, once he was out of earshot.

"For what?" I asked, in surprise.

"I wanted some alone-time with him. I could have stayed here while he helped you with that thing in your car," she continued, then a smile spread across her face as Jack returned. "See you tomorrow, Jack," she said, in a cheery voice.

"Have a good night, Gemma."

"Hmm," she said, casting a dark glance at me.

I went to follow her out of the cottage, but Jack leant over and said in my ear: "You're still coming back for dinner, aren't you?"

I nodded and gave him a smile, then went to join Gemma.

CHAPTER EIGHTEEN

After spending the rest of the journey listening to Gemma gush over Jack and chide me for disrupting her plans, I was glad when we reached her place and she got out the car.

"Well, have a good holiday," she said, peering through the window. "Bring something back. A Spanish hunk, or two."

"Two?" I said, smiling. "I thought you were all about Jack?"

"I am," she said, then winked. "But there's nothing in the rule book about appreciating the male form."

I laughed. "Never change, Gemma."

"Don't plan to. Bye, Carla. Thanks for the lift." She gazed at the snow cascading down, and rushed towards her front door.

I turned the car around and drove back to Jack's. Finally.

Five minutes later I was knocking on his door, regretting not having brought any gloves.

"Come in!" I heard him say.

I stepped inside. The hallway was in darkness, but there was light coming through from the living room, so I took off my coat, hung it up and went in search of Jack.

He was in the kitchen, serving the stew onto two plates. The table had been set, with a three-tiered candle sat aglow in the centre. So much for him not being a romantic. But my attention had been taken by the fluffy red dressing gown Jack wore. His hair was wet and swept back. It suited him.

"I go away for five minutes..." I joked.

"Thought I'd jump in the shower while you were gone," he explained.

I leant on the counter next to the plates. "Must have been a quick shower."

"I could always finish it after dinner. Might need someone to help me, though..." He let the sentence linger as he took the plates across to the table.

"Yes, I'm sure I could give you a number for Home Help," I said, inhaling the smells emitting from the table. As well as the stew, there was a bowl of roasted, herbed veg and another bowl of mashed potato. My belly growled with appreciation.

"Well," Jack said, taking the empty pot back to the counter. "Take a seat and fill your boots."

"You not going to get changed?" I asked, sitting down.

"Good idea. I'll just be a minute. Don't wait on me." He sped out the door and returned a few minutes later in a cable-knitted jumper and jeans, and bare feet.

"Very highland man-esque," I said, as he took a bottle of wine from the wine rack and brought it over to the table.

He looked down at his jumper and chuckled. "Oh, yeah. I bought this in London before I came up here the first time. Thought I'd need something warm with the notorious Scottish weather."

"Yeah, it's not quite the weather for bikinis and briefs," I concurred.

"That reminds me," Jack said, pouring us both a glass of wine, before settling down into the chair opposite. "Will you be wearing a bikini on holiday?"

"Might do," I lied. "Why?" I leant forward, chin in hand, wondering where this was leading, though I could have a good guess.

"Oh, no reason. Just wanted to have a good image of you when I think about how you're getting on in Spain."

"You're a creep," I laughed, leaning back.

"I see myself more of a caring boyfriend."

"Oh, so you're my boyfriend, are you?" I asked, pretending to be shocked.

"How very presumptuous of you," he replied. "Who said I was *your* boyfriend?"

"Yes, you're right. How remiss of me. Phew! I can head to Spain safe in the knowledge that I *don't* have a boyfriend, then." I smiled smugly and took a bite of the stew.

"Okay, okay," Jack said, raising a hand in defeat. "Since I am such a gentleman, I will allow you to tell people - especially macho Spanish guys - that I *am* your boyfriend."

I nodded. "That *is* very gentlemanly of you."

"And caring, don't forget."

"*And* caring. Like a caring boyfriend."

"Exactly." He jabbed the air with his fork.

We finished the meal, snuggled up on the sofa for a bit, then decided it was time to get the Dalek back to mine. The sky was pitch black, and the snow lay heavy on the ground. If we'd left it any longer, nobody would be going anywhere.

With a bit of a struggle we made it back to mine and got the metallic villain indoors just after 9pm. Then Jack stayed over - well, it would have been silly to walk back in that kind of weather, wouldn't it?

The next morning I woke to the shriek of my phone as the alarm went off. Someday I would get around to going through the options and pick something less shrill. I nudged Jack awake and told him he'd have to leave soon. He asked if he could have a quick shower... then asked, with a wicked look, if I wanted to join him. Tempted as I was, I had too much to do and told him I'd have my shower after him.

The taxi arrived at 8am to take me to Inverness, where I was to get a coach to Glasgow. The girls would be there to greet me, and then onwards to the airport.

"I'll miss you," Jack said, grabbing my waist and pulling me to him, as the taxi driver lifted my case into the boot of the car.

"Me too," I whispered back, and gave him a brief but deep kiss. "Gotta run."

He cut a desolate figure as we pulled away from the house. I regretted the timing of him and I hooking up. At least he'd be there when I returned. That's unless Gemma tempted him away while I was gone.

On the coach from Inverness to Glasgow, I sent the girls a message. We had a Chat Group on social media where we'd keep up to date with each other's lives. It also came in handy for arranging holidays, too.

On the coach now. Still meeting me off the bus?

Meena was the first to message back. *Course! Can't wait to see you in person. Been bloody ages, lass!*

I smiled. Meena was the first person I made friends with at high school, after we both got lost on our second day trying to find the French department. Born in Yorkshire, Meena and her family moved to Scotland when she was 12. Then Meena went back down south to study at Sheffield university. She was the Girly I'd seen the least of, since I'd moved north.

I was just about to reply when a text message notification appeared on my screen. I swiped it away and finished my message. I was officially on holiday and the next seven days were all about me and my friends, who I'd neglected for far too long.

Half an hour later, Meena and I had dissected the contents of our suitcases, our plans for dealing with any unwanted attention, and our firm decision *not* to stick to the tourist-trap places. I checked the text message I'd been sent and noticed it was from Jack.

At least we'll always have the Dalek... Have a brilliant time. Jack x

I smiled, but didn't reply straight away. Instead, I put my phone back in my bag and took in the wintery scenery outside my window.

Arriving at Glasgow bus station, I was ready for a good stretch of my arms and legs. Meena, Kelly, Louisa and Kate were all standing there, peering at different buses pulling into the depot. I waved frantically out of the window, noting Louisa's new life as a blonde.

"Omigod!" Meena squealed, wrapping her arms around me before I'd even got a decent distance away from the bus. "Look at you! The highlands is obviously working its magic on you!"

"I could say the same about Sheffield," I remarked. "Looking good, kid."

"Always," She said, pretending to preen.

I embraced the rest of the gang, and Kate - always the most organised out of us all - sought a taxi to take us to the airport. As I got updated on everyone's lives - snippets of which I knew about from our social media messaging - I wondered if I should tell them about Jack.

All thoughts of Gemma, the money, the Dalek - and a few times, even Jack - disappeared during our stint in Spain. It felt lovely to be under the heat of the sun and, with some coaxing from the girls, I even bought a bikini from a branch of Gap, and donned it during our one day's sunbathing session on the beach. We received some attention from guys, I'll admit, but Louise and Meena have such fantastic figures, the gazes would inevitably end with them.

And yes, I got chatted up in a bar during our second-last evening abroad. His name was Steve, here on a stag weekend with his mates ("I'm not the groom, by the way"), and tea-total. He'd grown bored with his friends' drunken antics so had found himself in this bar. Steve was nice, even when I told him about Jack. He just wanted to have a chat with someone sober, but his attention coolled off notably after mention of the boyfriend. So much so that he upped and left halfway through a conversation. The next time I saw him he had his tongue stuck down another woman's throat.

On our last night, we had a nice meal at a nearby restaurant. During the past six days we'd kept talk of dating and relationships to a minimum; our mantra being "It's all about The Girlies". But during the main course, Kelly brought up the guy she'd started seeing, which in turn saw Louisa discuss her forthcoming divorce. After Meena and Kate had their turn, all eyes fell on me.

"No man on the horizon, Car?" Meena asked. "Or woman. You might have got sick of men like Louisa, here."

"Best decision I ever made," Louisa added, raising her glass.

"No women," I said. "Men? Well..." I let the rest of the sentence linger, as eyes widened and eyebrows rose.

CHAPTER NINETEEN

It was like I had never left when I returned to Auchtermachen. Even as I entered the cold, empty house the memories of Spain were beginning to fade. Thankfully there were plenty of photographic evidence of the holiday. The snow had melted, but the house was freezing cold. I stuck the heating on then filled the kettle, giving a nod to the Dalek in the living room as I switched on the TV.

I hadn't switched my phone on since boarding the plane in Barcelona. I promised Meena I'd let them know I arrived home safely, so turned it on. The phone immediately went scatty with notifications. The majority of them were annoying social media alerts. One was a text from Pete, hoping I was having a great time. Three messages were from Jack. The first reiterating how much he was missing me. The second consisted of two photos - a close-up of his face pouting, and a selfie of him in his Heartthrob get-up, blowing a kiss. The third one had been sent an hour earlier.

What time do you get home? Want some company? Missed you like mad. Jack x

I texted back: *Just got in. Tired but get your arse round here, anyway. x*

The BBC ten o'clock news had just started on the television. I felt guilty asking him to come round at this time of night, but he was the one to suggest visiting in the first place.

The phone went again. *On my way. x*

When he arrived, I surprised myself by greeting him with an urgent, desperate kiss that - as we moved further into the house - evolved into slow and deep, and utterly sexy. I hadn't realised just how much I'd missed him. Absence makes the heart grow fonder? It also makes you utterly turned-on, too. Clothes were discarded, the bedroom was sought, and we never came up for air for another half hour.

"Wow" was the first coherent word Jack spoke, as we both got our breath back under the duvet. "That was... intense."

"Yeah, sorry about that," I said.

He shook his head. "Never apologise."

"Okay, I won't." I shifted onto my side and traced my fingers along his chest. "Hi, by the way."

He laughed and covered my hand with his own. "Hi. Nice holiday?"

"It was great. Loved spending time with the girls. We're thinking of meeting up in the new year."

"In Spain?"

"No, we straddle the UK, so somewhere central we can all reach easily." I felt a hand stroke my thigh.

"Did you have to use the word 'straddle' while I still have a hard-on? I'm getting flashbacks, Missy."

"I aim to tease," I replied, moving his hand round to the back.

"Oh, you're in trouble now."

In one movement, I was lying on my back, with Jack looming over me, eyes narrowed. "You better find something to hold on to," he warned, before his head disappeared under the duvet.

On my first day back at work, I awoke not to my alarm, but with a kiss and a plate of scrambled eggs on toast and a hot cup of tea.

"You need to stay over more often," I told Jack, now dressed and opening the curtains.

He came back to the bed, kissing my forehead, sat on the side. "You needed a decent sleep. There's enough hot water for a shower."

"Thanks. You working today?"

"Day off. Did an extra day last Friday. Client had a headache, so filming was halted until she felt better."

"It's Pete's birthday today."

"Happy birthday, old man." Jack raised his cup in a toast.

"The company have bought a cake for him, so I think we're having that around three. Then everyone's coming here where he can get his Dalek and we can have drinks and nibbles."

Jack paused "You did just say 'nibbles' and not..."

"I said nibbles," I said, noting I was naked under the duvet. "Don't tell me you're still turned-on."

"I'm always turned-on, around you." He reached across and we kissed briefly. "But I don't have time for you to have your wicked way with me, again. I'm house-hunting, today."

"Are there any houses for sale in the village?"

"Only ones I could never afford. I'm was thinking something in Inverness. It's not London, but it's less rural and out of the way than here."

A small part of me felt defensive about the village. But Jack was a city boy, and Inverness was a sort of halfway house between London and Auchtermachen.

Jack looked at his watch. "In fact, I'm viewing a flat at half eleven. I need to head home first."

"Want a lift?" I asked, finishing the last of the toast. "I can have a quick shower."

"Thanks, but it's a nice day. I'll walk it. What time should I get here for Pete's bash?"

"Well, I could do with a hand getting everything ready. I've told people to be here for 6pm, so... four?"

"Two hours to fool around? Sounds good."

"Two hours to get everything ready," I corrected him. "Though if we finish early..."

"I'll make sure of it," Jack said, with a wink.

We kissed again

"Go," I said, nudging him away. "Go find a place in Inverness I can roam naked in."

"Okay!" He rushed out of the room, then yelled "See you later" before leaving the house.

Since Pete's editing room was on the small side, a little get-together was planned for one of the unused meeting rooms on the third floor. I'd bought two large cakes from the supermarket and hoped there'd be enough for those that showed up.

Being one of Pete's oldest friends at Highland Fling I thought I'd be saying a few words about the birthday boy, before inviting him to cut the cake. However, Hazel sought me out beforehand and told me she'd been given the task by HR, and that she hoped I didn't mind.

"Course not," I said, truthfully. Then added. "The party's still being held at mine, isn't it?"

"As far as I know, yes," Hazel replied. "Besides, my place is far too tiny for everyone to cram themselves into. What did we all buy him, anyway?" When I told her, she looked surprised at first but then gave me a thumbs-up. "He was talking about always wanting one of those, the other night. He'll love it."

"I hope so," I said, not missing the mention of 'the other night'. So they still met up after work, did they?

It seemed a lot of people were in need of cake, come three o'clock. So much so that the room was packed fairly quickly. Pete was already there with Hazel, and I saw a look of surprise on his face at the amount of people filing in. I made my way towards them.

"Good turn-out," I said, as more people drifted in.

Hazel looked worried. "I don't think there'll be enough cake to go around."

"It'll have to be really thin slices," said Pete.

"Once it's gone, it's gone. Anyway, there'll be cake at your surprise party tonight," I reassured him.

"Surprise party? And you're telling him now?" Hazel asked.

Pete looked at her. "Hazel, everyone here has a party thrown for their birthday, every year. I assumed it wouldn't be any different for me. Anyway, we better crack on. I don't think we can fit anymore in here."

I stood with the crowd as Hazel got everyone's attention. Pete stood next to her, staring down at the two chocolate cakes and listening to the compliments raining down on him.

After the cakes had been cut and slices handed out, everyone formed into their usual groupings and chatted for a while. Hazel had a phone meeting so had to leave early. I found Pete talking to Violetta, one of the camera crew, who was finishing her bit of cake.

"Happy birthday." I gave Pete a peck on the cheek.

"I was just telling Pete I can't make his party tonight," Violetta explained. "My brother and his family from back home are arriving tonight. But I want to hear all the juicy gossip to-morrow."

"You make it sound like it'll be an orgy," Pete exclaimed.

"It better not be, not if I can't go. Anyway, I better get back."

We watched the small woman leave, then exchanged looks.

"Well," began Pete, with a chuckle. "The things you learn about people."

"She was joking. I think. How are you, anyway? Haven't had a chance to catch up since I got back."

"Oh, you know. Same old, same old. How was Spain?"

"Brilliant. It was great to get away for a bit."

"Listen, I don't mean to pry but how's it going with you and lover boy?"

I hesitated. "Good. Great, in fact."

Pete looked surprised. "Really? Well, good for you. I'm only asking 'cos Gemma seems to have been cosying up to him. Or trying to, anyway."

"I thought she would." This was silly. I needed to tell her Jack was off-limits. I thought he might have done it for me.

"And you're fine with that?" Pete continued.

"Not a hundred percent, no," I admitted.

"She doesn't know about you and Jack, does she?"

I shook my head. "Not yet."

"Best get her told, then. Before she embarrasses herself even more."

CHAPTER TWENTY

With Jack's help, the Dalek was shifted into my bedroom where it would be wheeled out at the right moment. The food was all laid out on the kitchen table and counters. I'd run out of plates so was now using bowls and whatever came to hand. I'd planned to make a soundtrack to play during the party, but I ran out of time so hooked Spotify up to my bluetooth speakers, and chose a 60s-80s playlist.

"Anything else need done?" Jack asked, looking around the living room. We'd put up some balloons in the corners of the ceiling and I'd sourced a *Birthday* banner from the post office.

"I think that's it," I declared.

"Good." Jack moved towards me and wrapped his arms around my waist. "So we *do* have time to fool around."

"Sorry, but I need to get changed, first and I'm not messing up my make-up for anyone."

"Aw, you're no fun anymore," he said, then tapping me lightly on the arse and released me.

"It's half five. You may as well have a drink and relax. People will start arriving soon."

I was showered, changed and applying some mascara when Jack shouted through that there was someone at the door.

"Just answer it," I shouted back. "I'll be there in a second."

When I came through there were seven people, cradling glasses of wine and helping themselves to nibbles, including Gemma. Her eyes lit up when I entered the kitchen.

"Caz! You look great!"

I was immediately suspicious. She sounded too chirpy, and I was only wearing a pair of black jeans and a teal shirt. "So do you," I answered. And she did. Her hair was styled. Her make-up was subtle for a change. It took years off her.

"Thanks," she said, glancing at the floor briefly. "Um, Jack answered the door."

"Yup, he did."

"I take it he was the first to arrive." The way she was looking at me was slightly unnerving.

"He was, yes." I really needed to tell her. "Gemma, look. Can we talk?"

"Aren't we?" she said breezily, reaching to take a blueberry muffin from a plate.

"We are, but this is something -"

"He's here!" Someone shouted out, and a cheer arose as Pete came into view, arriving with several others, including Hazel.

"Damn," I said. "Right, we'll speak later. Find me afterwards," I told Gemma.

She shrugged. "Okay."

Weaving my way through the bodies to where Pete was, I spotted Jack talking to Tessa. I had the duration of the party to tell Gemma about him and I. It was time to reveal Pete's present, so I tapped Jack on the shoulder and asked him to get ready to wheel the gift out.

After getting everyone to shush, I made an off-the-cuff speech about Pete which I think went down well.

"Now we'd like to give you a little something, Pete, to show how much we appreciate you. I We hope you like it, even if it does try to exterminate you."

"Jesus Christ!" Pete exclaimed, as Jack brought through the life-size villain. The crowd parted to allow them past. "How much did this set you back?" he asked, touching and staring at the thing, in genuine shock.

"We had enough," I said, exchanging smiles with Jack.

"Th-thank you," Pete stammered. "Thank you, everyone!"

A cheer went up and everyone applauded. Then some drifted off towards the kitchen in search of more food and drink. Others surrounded the Dalek.

"He seems happy with it," Jack said, as we stood watching a beaming Pete impart his knowledge about the Doctor Who villains to anyone who would listen.

"Told you he would," I said, then noticed his glass was empty. "Want a top up?"

"Not yet. Need to make space. Back in a minute." I watched him head out into the hallway.

"Carla," Dave, one of the prop artists, approached me, carrying a ringing phone. "Found this on your bookcase." He dropped it into my hands and walked away. It was Jack's phone. Someone named The Hellhound was calling. I left it ringing. Jack would be back soon, and I didn't normally answer people's mobile phones. Unless in an emergency.

I spotted him talking to Pete. Pete had barely left the model's side since the reveal, as if it was in danger of trundling away.

"This is yours, I believe." I held the now-silent phone out to Jack.

"Thanks. Where did I leave it?" He checked the screen, and I saw the change of expression in his face.

"Not going to ring Hellhound back?" I teased.

Jack shook his head, a serious look on his face. "Not right now."

"So, I hear you two are getting along well," Pete said, taking a sip of wine.

Jack slipped an arm around my waist. "Yeah, we are, though Carla doesn't want a certain person to know."

"Gemma," said Pete.

"Got it in one," said Jack.

"It's not that I don't want her to know, it's just... complicated."

"You're being silly," said Jack. "Gemma's an adult. I know it will be a struggle, but she'll get over me."

"I hope so," I mutter.

People began leaving around 9. There were still half a dozen guests milling around. Gemma was drunk and blasting Lance's techniques as a lover to a clearly-embarrassed Hazel and Pete. There was no sign of Jack, and his phone was ringing on my bed.

"Jack?" I checked to see if he was hiding in my wardrobe, then checked the name flashing on the screen. The Hellhound again. I was about to answer when it rang off. I frowned. Where the heck *was* Jack?

I jumped as the phone sprang into life again. Flustered, I answered it. "Hello? Jack Jefferson's phone."

"Who the hell is this?" A familiar voice hissed. It was the Australian man from the other day. "Where's Jack?"

"I'm not sure," I said. "Can I take a message?"

"Who are you? One of his tarts, I suppose?"

My view of the caller had gone to wary apathy to downright hostility. "Who are *you*?" I countered, guessing his birth certificate didn't actually state Hellhound as a forename..

"I'm Rufus Murray, not that it's got anything to do with you, sweetheart. Tell Jack he better have not chickened out. I'm expecting a scoop on that bloody brothel on my desk by the end of the week."

Rufus Murray? But he was the owner of *The Daily Informer*...

"There are no brothels here. Sorry, you've been misinformed," I said, my throat suddenly dry..

"I mean that bloody Highlander Flings, or whatever it's called. Just tell him if he still wants to continue working for me, then I want that report!"

The call ended. With a shaking hand, I stared at the phone. Was this right? It had to be a joke, surely. Jack working for that rag? I dropped the device on the bed and pulled open the drawer of my bedside table. Underneath the Gaiman books and notepads, I found what I was looking for.

I hadn't planned to keep the newspaper, let alone the article. But I'd stuck the thing in the drawer, and it had laid there, ever since, gathering dust. My eyes scanned for the writer of the hatchet job. It's funny, I'd memorised the name ever since it had been published, but after that phone call, I couldn't recollect it at all. Just remembered it had been a male name.

Bernie Fraser. Not Jack Jefferson. At least that was something.

"Carla, there you are." Pete stood in the doorway. "I'm heading off soon. Just wanted to say thanks, for the present and everything."

"No problem." I picked up the paper again and went through it, page by page, in search of Jack's name.

"Everything okay?"

"I don't know," I answered, distracted by my quest. With my gaze jumping from article to article, I was feeling a little light-headed.

The next thing I knew, Pete was by my side, but I stayed focussed. I didn't want to believe it. That Jack had been lying to me all this time.

"What are you doing?" He asked, in a gentle voice.

"Possibly commiserating my shortest-ever relationship," I answered, before uttering a very strong swear word under my breath.

There, on page 19, under a headline about the ongoing sorry state of a minor celebrity, was 'Jack Jefferson'. There was even a small headshot of him.

"Carla," Pete continued. "What's going on?"

I folded the paper in half, thrust it into Pete's hand, and pointed to Jack's article.

"I don't understand," Pete started to say, then paused as his focus shifted to the small photograph. "Oh." He looked up at me. "So he used to work for the Informer?"

"I think he *still* works for the Informer," I tell him.

"Right. And I take it by the look on your face, he's never told you any of this."

"Got it in one."

"I don't know if he's still around. I haven't seen him in a while," said Pete.

Just as he'd finished speaking, the bedroom door was pushed open. There he was. The liar.

"Ello, ello, ello," he said, his jacket wet from the rain. "What's going on here, then?"

"You're leaving," I said, glaring at him.

His grin, once endearing and now irritating, fell. "Why? What's happened?"

"You've been busted, mate." Pete held out the newspaper to him, but I grabbed it instead and thrust the old photograph in Jack's face.

"Rufus Murray wants your report on his desk," I said, amazed at how calm I sounded. "Better do what your boss says."

Jack took the newspaper but didn't look at it. "Carla, let me explain -"

"No need, Jack. I know. I can put two and two together and get lying bastard. Just go."

Pete got to his feet. "Come on, mate. The party's over."

"No, *mate*," Jack told him. "I'm not going anywhere. Not until I've spoken to Carla. In private."

"I don't want to hear it. Just take your phone and get lost." I scooped up the mobile phone from the bed, and threw it to him.

He caught it, and stared at the thing for a moment. "So that's it? You won't hear what I have to say?"

"Finally he gets it."

Dejected, he slid the phone into his jacket pocket, and left without another word.

"I'll see you out," Pete said, following him.

I stood there, alone. I couldn't believe it. Couldn't believe Jack had conned me like that. I knew it had been too easy. Mr Right doesn't just fall into your lap. There is always a catch. And I'd discovered that Jack Jefferson was far from 'the one'.

Someone filled the doorway. Gemma, glass in hand and tipsy, leaning against the door frame. "Cazza, Hazel says you and Jack are an item. Whatsallthatbout?" She slurred.

"She's mistaken, Gemma." I kept my voice light. "There is definitely nothing between Jack and I."

Gemma peered at me for a second, then pushed herself upright. "Good," she said, before wobbling back down the hallway..

CHAPTER TWENTY-ONE

I didn't sleep well that night. Well, how could I? All I could think about was how much of a fool I was. I mean, the signs were there. I'd just assumed he had a terrible taste in newspapers, but he would have been checking out the dreich his colleagues were making up. And now I was going over everything, it made sense how Jack knew about the wife of his boss being a client of Highland Fling.

I was angry. Angry at him, angry at myself for not sticking to my guns and leaving things well alone after that one-night stand. Gemma was welcome to him. She had dismissed the original article as a load of crap, so maybe she wouldn't mind that Jack worked for a company that could have jeopardised her job.

It was almost 3am, and my alarm would go off in a few hours, so I got up and, making a cup of tea, curled up in the Snug and decided what I would do next. As far as I was aware, only Pete and I knew about Jack's subterfuge. Part of me wanted to stride right into HR at 9am and reveal all. Get Jack fired. I mean, why would they keep him on when he was only there to dig for anything he could twist and mould into something sensational for that poor excuse for a newspaper?

Six hours later, it was still preying on my mind as I walked into work. Pierre greeted me, from behind the reception desk, with his usual pleasantries. Distracted, I offered him a half-hearted "Morning" before heading for the lifts.

Inside, my finger hovered before the second and third floor buttons. My office or HR? Go straight to Tessa or ponder on what to do, further.

"Good morning." One of the suited executives, who had never learnt my name, entered the lift and hit the button marked '3'. "Which floor?" he asked, ready to jab the panel again.

I told him I was heading for the same floor, so he busied himself on the five second journey flattening down his suit jacket and making no attempt at small talk. Arriving on the third floor, he gave up a brief smile then swept along the length of the corridor to his office where he did God knows what.

My legs took me in the opposite direction, towards the room at the end. Each passing second I spent wondering if I was doing the correct thing. Right until I knocked on the door. My decision made.

I walked in to an empty room. Typical. I thought about waiting, but Tessa and Terry often worked from home. I could have waited a very long time. One day made no difference.

I turned to go, and was almost knocked over by someone coming in.

"Oh, hello." Pete held a sheet of paper and looked surprised to see me. "No one in yet?" He asked, glancing around the room.

I shook my head. "Doesn't look like it."

"I'll just leave this here," he said, putting the paper down on Tessa's desk. "There's an issue with booking my holidays on the computer, so for now I'm back to using forms."

"Old school," I commented.

Pete made no attempt to leave. I knew what was coming.

"How are you?" he asked.

I let out a heavy sigh. "Fine, I suppose. Apart from feeling like an idiot."

"You weren't to know," Pete replied. Then after a pause, said: "Have you spoken to him this morning?"

"Haven't seen him. Don't want to, either."

"So you don't want to hear his side of the story?"

I looked at Pete, in surprise. "I don't need to. He's only here undercover for this stupid report he's writing."

"I don't get it, though," admitted Pete. "They've already written something about us. Why do it again? And why so secretive?"

I shrugged. "Rufus Murray's wife is one of our clients. Or was. That man certainly holds a grudge. He obviously wasn't content with the last article. Now he must be hungry for any dirt his *lackey* can dig up."

Pete watched me for a moment, then sighed and walked over to the door. "How come you're in here, anyway?"

I bit the inside of my lip. A bad habit, I know, but we all have them. "I was coming to tell HR about Jack. The sooner they know, the better."

"Have you told anyone else?" Pete asked.

"Only you and I know, for the moment."

He shut the door and spoken in a quiet voice. "Then I think you need to speak to Jack before you do anything else. Have all the facts first."

"He's a journalist!" I said, a little louder than I meant. "A journalist for one of the worst tabloids ever. He's a professional liar. He'll just twist things. You know what? It's good I found out this way, because he sure as hell, wasn't going to confess."

"Just take my advice," Pete repeated. "Speak to him. And if he really is a conniving little shitbag, then I'll back you up when you speak to Tess."

"Fine," I said reluctantly.

We left the room and came face to face with the HR manager who almost collided with us as she was busy rummaging through one of three bags.

"Oh hello you two," she said, standing upright. "Looking for me? Terry's in London. *Again*. Honestly, he always gets the cushy jobs. What can I do for you?"

"I was just handing my holiday form in," explained Pete.

"Uh-huh. Carla?" Tess's dark eyes landed on me.

I hesitated. "I was just chatting to Pete."

"Okay, well if there's nothing else..." said Tessa, moving past us and into her office. Pete and I wandered back along the corridor. I left him watching me enter the lift.

"Speak to him, okay," Pete said, searching my face for confirmation.

I nodded.

When I heard that Jack had called in sick, later on that morning, I was both relieved - that I didn't have to face him - and unsurprised that he was too chicken to face me.

"He's maybe got a hangover," said Gemma, who I was a little surprised to see was not visibly affected by the drinking she had done the previous night. She actually looked in rude health. "He'd better be here tomorrow. The next *Incident* is in two days' time, and if we need to tweak the fittings, I'd rather get it done sooner than at the last minute."

The *Incident* was what Highland Fling used to describe the clients' initial arrival in the 18th century. What happened was the client would get a treatment of choice in the small spa building a mile from HQ, then the beauty therapist would leave. When the client cottoned on that no one was coming to collect them, they would stumble out of the cabin, find themselves in 18th century Scotland and encounter their Highland Heartthrob for the first time. Yeah, sounds a wee bit contrived, I know.

Back at my desk I emailed Pete to make arrangements for getting his present back to his. While I waited for his response, I checked my phone on the off-chance Jack had sent a message. Nothing. Good.

I saved then closed the spreadsheet on my screen, and opened the browser, before typing **Jack Jefferson** and **Daily Informer**. Less than a hundred results. Several on the first page were courtesy of a spy novelist called Jack Jeffers.

After much scrolling, I started finding articles written by Jack. Celeb garbage that was the *Informer*'s usual bread and butter. A small part of me had hoped he'd been a chink of gold in a row of rotten teeth; a moral, self-aware journalist. But no. Clicking onto a link at random I found a hatchet piece on a TV cook caught speeding. Every tiny misdemeanour in their life was mentioned, almost with glee. I closed the tab. I'd never claimed to know Jack in-and-out - that's what dating was for - but I really didn't know him at all.

CHAPTER TWENTY-TWO

I was a little late leaving work that day. At five to five, just as I was about to switch down the computer, Terry phoned from London, asking if I could scan and email a *Highland Fling* brochure he had forgot to take. He had tried to get hold of Tessa, but she wasn't answering, and he needed the marketing piece urgently. So it was almost half an hour later when I drove out of the car park.

I'd already sent Pete a text telling him I'd be late. He'd finished at mid-day; and would be at mine for half-past five so we could finally get the Dalek to its final destination. The sky was clear blue and there was a nice warmth to the air, so I didn't feel guilty that he would have to wait outside the house.

I had a sudden need for fish and chips - the chippie, *Sizzle and Sauce*, always did a great takeaway. Turning the bend that would take me to the house, I'd see if Pete wanted something, too..

I spotted him sitting on the old weather-worn bench outside the house, talking to someone in a hooded jacket. One of the positives of living in a small community was the general friendliness to one another. It was rare you'd pass anyone in the street without them greeting you with a "hello" or a smile.

My fond grin turned to a grimace as I realised who it was.

I parked in the usual spot and readied myself as I got out the car.

"Made it then?" said Pete, getting to his feet.

"What's he doing here?" I said, refusing to look at the other man.

"We need to talk, Carla," Jack said. "Properly."

"Are you a reporter for the *Informer*?" I asked bluntly, taking the house keys out of my coat pocket and heading for the front door.

"Yes, but -"

"Then we have nothing further to say to each other," I interrupted. "Come in, Pete." I unlocked the door and stepped inside.

"Carla..." Pete started. "Just listen to the man, will you?"

"I don't need to. Are you coming in, or is this Dalek staying here forever?" I asked.

"Want a hand?" Jack asked, though I noticed he was addressing Pete.

Wise enough to gauge my reaction first, Pete shook his head. "Thanks, mate. I think we'll be okay."

"Fine."

I watched Jack as I kept the door open for Pete. He shoved his hands in his pockets, and head bowed, walked away.

As soon as I closed the door behind us, Pete rounded on me.

"You were a bit abrupt with him."

"And you seemed quite pally with him," I replied. "Nice chat, was it?"

We headed through to the kitchen where I stuck the kettle on. Pete sat down at the table and slipped off his jacket, hanging it over the back of the chair next to him. "I don't know why you're being so stubborn," he said, finally.

"The man lied, Pete. To all of us." Why didn't he seem to understand this? "It's one thing to do that, but the fact he was here undercover. To write another scathing article. It's disgusting."

"It was, by the way."

He'd lost me. "It *was* disgusting?"

"A nice chat. Me and Jack. He cares about you, you know."

"Yeah, great way of showing it," I answered. "I should have just told Tessa when I had the chance."

"Why didn't you?" Pete asked.

I didn't know. I was so angry. The question was why wasn't Pete?

"That's simple," he said, when I asked him. "I wasn't sleeping with him. He lied to you - personally *and* professionally. Of course you're raging."

"So what should I do?" I asked, flopping down on the chair next to him. "Just keep quiet? Let him write his sordid little story?"

"He won't be writing anything. He's been found out. His cover's blown."

"So he'll just quit and go back to London? Good."

"I guess so."

"What did he say? When you had your 'nice chat' out there?"

"He says he's made a mess of things. Asked me to speak to you. Get you to let him explain. For what it's worth, he seemed genuinely sorry."

"He's a good actor," I said dismissively.

"Should we get going?" Pete asked, getting up again.

"I thought we could have a cuppa first," I said. The kettle had just finished boiling.

"Have one at mine. We'll need it after lugging that thing indoors."

When I looked back, Pete was on his phone texting.

"Messaging Hazel?" I asked, glad to change the conversation at last.

"What makes you think that?" He asked, eyes not shifting from the screen, as his forefinger jabbed away.

I smiled. "Oh, nothing. You two seem very chummy, these days."

Pete shrugged as he finished his message and put away the phone. "I suppose so."

"Oh, come on," I said. "*You* know all about *my* love life. What about yours?"

I must admit, he didn't look impressed. But just as I was going to tell him to forget it, and that we should get going, he continued. "I don't have a love life. Hazel and me. It's not like that."

"Like what?" I asked, trying to wiggle my eyebrows.

"If you must know, we're starting up our own company."

I gaped at him. "Really?"

"Aye, now can we get going? We have work tomorrow."

After we'd got the Dalek into the boot and were on the road, I hit Pete with a ton of questions about his new business venture.

"A production company? Wow, that's great!" I said, once he'd revealed all.

"It'll *eventually* be a production company," Pete corrected. "At the moment, it's just a scriptwriter-"

"Hazel."

"- and an editor."

"You."

"We're starting small. Hazel's written a few monologues. We've done a couple of tests. Nothing more. As I say, it's still early days yet."

"It doesn't matter. Just remember me when you win your first BAFTA. What's the company called?"

"Haze and Peat Productions," he said, and spelt it out.

"Clever," I said. "So that's what you and Hazel have been up to. And I thought you guys were dating."

"She's seeing someone else," said Pete. I glanced at him, his face flushing slightly. Poor guy.

"Hey, you're not leaving Highland Fling, are you?"

"At some point in the future, yes. Don't get me wrong. It's a good company to work for. The people are nice enough."

"Thank you."

"But I'm not getting any younger, and I need to do something more satisfying - challenging - with my life before it's too late."

"I don't blame you," I said. "I feel like that, too, sometimes."

"You've no excuse. You're still a young thing."

"I suppose compared to old people like you, I am."

"Cheeky."

We drove on, round the uphill slalom that was the road to Pete's place, the middle of a row of three houses. I parked up outside. As we manhandled the large figure of the Dalek into his house, I noticed a woman was watching through a neighbouring kitchen window, as she did the dishes. There was a look of confusion on her face.

"She's alright," Pete said, following my gaze. "It's her husband who's the nosy bugger." He gave her a brief wave as he neared the front door. The woman smiled, then moved away from the window.

We managed to get the model into the house and into the spare room on the ground floor where Pete kept all his science fiction memorabilia.

"You could open your own shop," I said, glancing at a shelf of Star Wars figurines and Blake 7 video cassettes.

"That's my back-up plan if Haze & Peat doesn't work out. Now, how about that cuppa?"

"Ooh, yes please," I said, rubbing my cold hands. "Do you want me to pop to the chippy and get us something to eat, too?"

"Uh, yeah. Alright. I'll come with you, though."

We headed back out. It hadn't snowed in a few days, and the blanket of white was giving away to icy slush. At least the Spring wasn't long in coming now. Oh, and how glorious Auchtermachen looked under the March sun.

Sizzle and Sauce was empty so we were served immediately. There was a moment of confusion when Pete ordered two fish suppers for himself.

"I'm hungry," he shrugged in reply.

Who was I to stand in the way of the man's stomach? Once I'd paid for my haggis supper, we returned to Pete's.

In the kitchen, he busied himself getting plates and cutlery for us both. I stuck the kettle on, and got the cups and tea bags ready.

"Invited someone else?" I asked, noting the three placemats on the table. "Not Hazel, by any chance?" I teased.

Someone knocked on the front door.

"Ah, perfect timing." Pete left the three suppers on the table and went to greet his guest.

I took another cup from the cupboard. At least with Hazel here, I'd get more information about their new company. I wondered if it was too early for them to hire an assistant.

It wasn't Hazel. The figure entered the kitchen, followed swiftly by Pete who gave me a beaming smile. "Look who it is."

"You planned this," I said, the extra fish supper and table setting clicking into place. I was tempted to walk out and go home. The only thing stopping me was the smell of the food Pete was placing on the table.

"Yes, I invited Jack," said Pete. "You two need to talk, and you won't do it off your own back," he added, giving me an admonishing look. "Tell you what, I'll take my chippy through to the living room. One of my programme's about to start, anyway. You two sit through here and *talk*."

"Cheers, mate," said Jack, as Pete scooped up his plate of fish and chips and walked into the other room.

"Well, this is awkward," I said with a sigh, sitting down.

"Yeah." Jack took the only other chair at the table and looked over the food.

"Pete got it, not me. If you don't like fish suppers, you'll have to see if he has anything else," I said.

"No, it's great. Thanks."

"Thank, Pete," I said, not maintaining eye contact with him. "So, start talking," I said, cutting into the haggis and taking a bite.

"I don't know where to start."

"Strange that, considering you've been desperate to speak to me since last night. And now you can't think what to say?"

"I know. Silly, isn't it?" He half-laughed.

I frowned and made myself look across at him. *Glared* would be a better description. "I don't find that funny."

"Sorry."

"Okay, since you're struggling to find the words, I'll help you. I'm sure you can answer 'yes' or 'no' to a few questions."

"Alright."

"Do you write for *The Daily Informer*?"

"Yes."

"Did you apply for a job at *Highland Fling* to write a warts-and-all article?"

"I wouldn't say-"

"Just a yes or no will suffice."

A sigh. "Yes."

"Right." I pushed back my chair and took one last chip from the plate. Hunger be damned.

"Where are you going?" he asked, looking up at me with one chip between his fingers.

"Home. I don't need to hear any more."

"Just sit down, will you?" Jack said, keeping his eyes on me. "Please."

"Fine," I said, dropping back down on the chair again. "But once I finish this, then I'm gone. And I'm a fast eater."

"Thank you." He ate the chip, then pushed his plate away so he could rest his folded arms on the table. "Yes, my boss sent me here to get any salacious stories I could on the company. Since Bernie wrote that article, Murray's wife has been back here. He wanted to print something that would destroy Highland Fling's reputation."

"Why didn't he just ask her not to go?" I asked.

"He did, apparently. She said she wouldn't, but she lied."

"So instead of speaking to her again, or divorcing - if the marriage is already on the rocks - he kills the company instead?"

"He's a man-child. Any normal person would do either of those things, but he's not normal. I volunteered for the job. I mean, to come here and write the article. But only because I knew you lived in the village. I thought I'd get to see you again. If I'd known you *worked* for Highland Fling..."

"What?" I asked, coldly. "You wouldn't have volunteered? Applied for a job here? Slept with me again?" My voice had risen, but I didn't care.

"I hate my job."

"Which one?"

"The journalist one. Well, I don't *hate* being a journalist. I didn't start off wanting to write fake news on the whim of a pathetic old man. I wrote pieces about the environment, politics and poverty. Important pieces."

"That's your own fault."

"You're right. I could have kept my integrity. I told you the truth when I first met you. I didn't like my job. I came up here for a break. To decide what to do with my life. When I woke up that morning, you weren't there. Then when I returned to London, it was like I'd never been away."

"I wasn't there? What's that got to do with anything? I hope you're not suggesting that if I'd stayed that morning, things would be different." I snorted.

"Who knows?" He said, then ate another chip.

"Jesus, don't you dare blame on me -" I started.

"I'm not. I'm just not explaining very well."

"You've got that right."

"Have you told anyone what you know? I've not had any angry calls from HR." He asked.

"Only Pete knows. For the moment."

There then followed an extremely tense and awkward silence between us that seemed to last far more than the few seconds it was.

He nodded. "Right." He studied me for a moment, then got to his feet. "Tell Pete thanks for the food." He paused, then continued. "I've explained all I can. It doesn't look like you're going to change your mind. Bye Carla."

He walked out, leaving me confused. I was supposed to be the one to walk out.

I heard the creak of the spare room door before Pete walked into the kitchen.

"Oh," he said, sounding surprised. "I thought you'd be the one to go."

I picked up a chip and looked at it. "So did I."

So there I was. Single again. I didn't have time to mourn (regret? celebrate?) my new status, though. The very next day I learned that Hollywood was coming to Highland Fling.

CHAPTER TWENTY-THREE

Alright, that was a teensy white lie. It wasn't Hollywood, but Britain's answer to it: the BBC. Our beloved HR co-manager, Terry, hadn't just been indulging in liquid lunches during his stay in London. He had been drumming up interest in the company and persuaded a sub-group of the documentary department of BBC Scotland to pay a visit.

The initial email was sent out by the CEO of Highland Fling, and by lunchtime everyone knew, and was busy gossiping about who would front the documentary, or if it would be some nameless reporter.

Hazel, Pete, Gemma and I clustered around the kitchenette, all supping from coffee cups and discussing the news. Pete was indulging in a mini-rant about the state of modern documentaries (something about fast cuts and intrusive music). The rest of us nodded in agreement, letting him get it off his chest.

"I wonder who they'll interview," said Gemma, frowning. "Selena, Terry or Tessa. The boys, obviously."

By 'the boys', she meant Stefan, the newly married Freddie and Jack. The Heartthrobs. Reminded of the lying toad, I realised that I hadn't seen him, all morning. Keeping a low profile, no doubt. Scared I'd reveal his secret.

"Oh god," said Hazel, lowering the cup from her lips for a second. "They're going to have to advertise again."

Gemma jerked her head round so quickly, I swear I heard bones crack. "What do you mean?"

"Oh." Hazel took in the three confused faces in front of her. "I thought you'd heard. Jack. He's quit."

Pete and I exchanged looks. I felt my skin prickle.

"Don't be silly," Gemma laughed. "He's not quit. He would have said something."

Hazel just shrugged. "I was with Tessa when she opened the letter. He's quit. Gone back to London. Says he's sorry for everything. Tessa's livid."

"But that makes no sense," said Gemma, swinging her - thankfully empty - cup rather carelessly. "I thought he liked it here. Told me he *loved* it here."

"A man can change his mind," said Pete.

"I'll call him," said Gemma, putting her cup on the side and charging down the corridor.

"I honestly thought everyone knew," said Hazel, watching Gemma as she disappeared into the lifts.

"It's not your fault," said Pete. "You know this place. We can only deal with one thing at a time, and this documentary business takes precedence."

"Poor Gemma," Hazel went on, unaware of what had gone on between Jack and I. "She really liked him."

Back in my office, I re-read the details about the documentary (it was a *long* email). Pete visited, carrying a plate with two slices of banana cake. He offered one to me as he sat in the chair opposite.

"Courtesy of Tessa. 'Cos of the BBC coming. There's a heap of doughnuts and gateau in the canteen."

"Thanks," I said. It was gone half-past three, but my belly was feeling a little empty.

"How are you?"

"I'm absolutely dandy. You *do* know you already asked how I was doing, this morning?"

"Ah, but that was before we found out lover boy had gone. So, I'll ask again: how are you?"

I looked at the slice of cake in my hand, studying it before taking a bite. "I'm alright," I said, in a smaller voice than I intended.

"How do you feel now that he's quit?"

"Relieved."

"Relieved?"

I nodded. "I don't have to tell them what he did. They don't *need* to know, now."

"They'll find out if he writes that article."

I stared at a crumb that had dropped onto the desk. "Crap," I said, softly. I looked up at Pete, searching for an answer. "Do you think he will?"

"I don't know, love. Sorry."

I leant back in my chair, defeated. I would have to tell them. At least they would be prepared, and it wouldn't come out of the blue like last time.

"For what it's worth, when he and I had a little chat the other day, he did seem genuinely remorseful at the whole mess. He said he hated his job at the newspaper."

"Yeah, he told me the same when I first met him," I said, then added. "Though he didn't say *what* his job was, exactly."

"Maybe you should contact him. Find out what *he's* planning to do, before *you* do anything."

"What a bloody mess," I said, massaging my temples as I felt the onset of a headache. I didn't want to contact him or see him ever again. I wasn't even sure why I still had his number in my phone contacts list.

"At least you found out when you did, if that's some small consolation."

"Can we talk about something else? How's Dalek Fred?"

"He's not tried to exterminate me yet; I think it's love."

That made me smile. "And how is Haze & Peat?"

"We're doing okay. Hazel's a bit miffed that we didn't think about doing a little video about this place ourselves."

"You still could, you know. Do a little video diary. A day in the life. You could always upload it to YouTube once the documentary goes out."

"Hark at you, full of ideas," teased Pete. "Anyway, it's not a dead cert the doc will go ahead, yet. They have to recce the place, first."

"Hark at you, using words like 'recce.'"

We ate our cake in silence.

"I'd best get back. I've got a big task on my hands." Pete wiped his trousers of any crumbs as he stood up.

"Oh yes?"

"Aye. Miss Featherstone has an uncanny ability to find all the discreet cameras and look directly at them all the time. I think she's more interested in being on film than in Stefan."

"Ugh, I hate when they do that. Good luck."

"You, too," he said pointedly, before leaving.

After work, a group of us went to The Thistled Inn. I noticed Gemma already nursing a drink, sitting alone and staring at her phone.

"Mind if I join you?" I asked, already placing my drink on the table and slipping off my coat.

"Sure," Gemma barely looked up from the small screen in her hand. I sensed conversation would be sparse.

"Busy day?" I asked, filling the silence.

Gemma shrugged. "Just the usual." She looked up. "Why's he not answering, Carla? What have I done?" She looked so despondent that I felt awful.

"You've not done anything," I reassured her. "He mustn't have liked the job, that's all."

"But he did. We were talking about it, the other day. Jack and I. He said he didn't realise how fun it was. He loved the village and everyone here. He seemed... giddy, to be honest. Are you trying to tell me he woke up one morning and changed his mind? Come on."

"Maybe something happened, and he had to return to London."

"That doesn't explain why he won't answer my calls or return my texts. I've sent seven, and he's not answered a single one. I've called and left messages five times. And nada."

"I don't know, Gemma. Men are weird." I took a sip of my drink and then tried to veer the conversation away from Jack. "So, the documentary sounds exciting, eh?"

"They'll have to replace him soon, if he's not coming back. With spring coming, we're booked up right through until September."

"I'm sure they'll sort it all out."

"What was Hazel talking about?"

The sudden turn in conversation confused me for a moment.

"What do you mean?"

"At Pete's party. She said you and Jack were together."

"Why did she say that?" I asked, as if it was a ridiculous notion.

"I don't know." Gemma looked at me through narrow eyes. *Oh god*, I thought. *This is where she adds two and two together and gets the correct answer.*

Her eyes flickered back and forth between mine as the machinations in her brain started working. I tensed up, waiting.

"Carla, are you sleeping with Jack?" she asked, carefully.

"No," I replied, easily. Then my shoulders sagged. "Not anymore."

"I bloody knew it!" Gemma exclaimed, slamming her hand down on the table, and getting a few looks in return. "I always knew there was something between you two. God, what an idiot!"

"I wanted to tell you," I said, nervously. "But there never seemed a good time."

"So you let me go around like some lovesick puppy. Jesus, Carla. You've made me look a right fool. I *told* you how I felt about him. And you still shagged him! God, you must have had a good laugh together over me," she hissed.

"It wasn't like that," I kept my voice low. "I met him way before he became a Heartthrob."

Gemma frowned. "Why didn't you say anything, then? You acted like you didn't know each other when I introduced you."

"I don't know. It was... awkward. I didn't expect to see him again."

"God, I really want to throw this drink over you, right now," Gemma said, her voice now calm. "Or hit you."

"Go ahead," I muttered. "I would in your position."

"For goodness's sake. Stop being a bloody martyr. I'm not going to hit you, or waste this drink on you." As if to prove it, she picked up her glass and drained the rest of the contents. She stood up. "One thing; are you the reason he's left?"

I thought about it for a moment. I'd discovered the truth, prompting him to leave. Go scurrying back to London with his tail between his legs and a backstabbing report in his hand. "Yes, but -" I said, ready to spill Jack's dirty little secret. But Gemma never stayed to listen, stalking out of the pub.

Pete was at the bar. He got my attention with a wave and held up an empty beer glass with a raise of the eyebrows.

I shook my head and headed home.

CHAPTER TWENTY-FOUR

That evening in the pub seemed to signal a new, rather lonelier period of my life. Gemma stopped talking to me unless it was strictly to do with work. Pete and Hazel spent all their spare time getting their production company off the ground. Our chats over a pint at *The Thistled Inn* became less frequent. Unless I'd arranged to meet Pete or Hazel, then I tended not to go out. This was where living in a small village was unbearable. Though no one in Auchtermachen knew the reason why Gemma and I were no longer speaking, the fact they knew what they knew in the first place, was irritating.

Spring arrived with a new generation of lambs and trees blossoming their coats of many colours. I still checked the contents of *The Daily Informer* for the inevitable piece on Highland Fling. Nothing so far, and I was thorough. Every morning I could be found in the newsagent's, checking each page of that rag. Bill, the newsagent, never said a word but I could tell he was miffed that I never bought a copy of the newspaper. And I never would.

One upside of having more time to myself was finding the time to chat with Meena and the others over the internet or on the phone. By mid-March we had a routine of group Skyping each Sunday evening and regaling one another with our adventures (or misadventures) during the week. They were all up to speed on my current single status, and like all good true friends, had wasted no time in ripping Jack a new one. They'd also declared they would boycott *The Daily Informer*. I'd thanked them, even though I knew none of them read that particular newspaper.

The documentary people had visited in February to scope the place out, and do an initial 'recce'. They were coming back in April and spending two weeks with us. The local hotels and B&Bs were quickly booked up, and a spruce-up of HQ was completed by the end of March. I'd even got a new chair for my desk!

Jack remained in my Contacts list l though I never called it, and received no calls from the number. I suppose I was waiting to see if he would try to get in touch. But as Meena told me, during one of our chat sessions, I could be waiting forever. I told her I'd delete it that night. I never did.

So I focussed all my attention on work. Spending most of my time cooped up in my office, only venturing out if absolutely necessary.

One such necessity was looking after a client who had become ill halfway through her stay. A stroke, in fact. I'd recognised the signs when I reached the building she was staying in. Freddie had been with her when it happened, and was able to alert someone immediately through the cameras.

An ambulance from Inverness picked her up and took her to hospital. I'd planned to go with her, but I'd only managed to raise one foot onto the vehicle when someone grabbed my arm and pulled me away.

"Sorry, Carla, but it's better if someone senior goes. It looks good." Tessa moved aside as the faceless, suited executive clambered aboard and sat to the side of the woman. The last vision I had of him as the doors closed, was of absolute irritation.

Once the ambulance had drove off, sirens blaring, the small group of people who had convened, broke away until it was just Freddie and I standing outside the mock-18th century dwelling.

"Poor Gladys," he remarked. "She was getting really into the storyline, too. I hope she's okay." His natural, soft Liverpudlian accent had replaced his impressive Scots.

"You raised the alarm early enough," I told him. "You've probably saved her life." I noticed he stood a little straighter at that.

"Christ, I'm freezing in this get-up," he remarked, rubbing his arms.

"You may as well change and go home. I don't think she'll be back anytime soon."

"Could do. But I need to stick around. Adam wanted some tips."

"He's still nervous, isn't he?" I asked. Adam was Jack's replacement; an actor whose highest profile part had been five minutes as a corpse in one of the last Taggart episodes.

"Yeah, poor lad. They've got him playing a jack-the-lad. They should write his character as a naïve, nervous wreck. The women would love it."

"You should suggest it," I said, as we set off back to HQ.

"Nobody listens to us," Freddie said. "We're not hired for our brains."

"How's married life?"

A smile appeared on his face. "Good. Not much has changed, really. Denise and I were together six years before the wedding."

"Why get married, then?"

He shrugged. "Why not?"

"Fair point," I replied.

We walked on, and soon HQ came into view. All glass front and looking like someone had just plonked a city office in the middle of nowhere. And then added a half-arsed car park, as an afterthought.

"Listen, I know it's none of my business but I just wanted to say I'm sorry to hear that things didn't work out between you and Jack."

"Sorry?"

"I know it wasn't common knowledge, your relationship."

"How did you -?" I began to ask, wondering just who else knew. Not that it mattered now.

"How did I know?"

I nodded. "Did Gemma tell you?"

"No. Even though I wasn't hired for my brain, I *do* still have one. Let's just say I picked up on things. Body language, that sort of thing."

"Right. Thanks for your... commiserations. To be honest, it was a lucky escape. He wasn't who I thought he was."

"You mean the newspaper thing?".

I stopped in my tracks. "You knew?"

"Yeah."

"And you didn't say a word?"

"Did you?"

"I was going to. I ended things with him as soon as I found out. What about you?"

"I didn't end things with him."

"Ha ha, you're such a comedian."

"I'd looked him up online. I always do with new starts. Helps to know the kind of person you're working alongside. Found some stuff linking him to the *Informer*, so I asked him about it," Freddie continued, with a shrug.

"He told you everything?"

"Eventually. Called me up the day after Pete's party and arranged to meet up for a pint. He spilt the beans, then.

"He was in an awful state. I think he needed someone to speak to. Listen, can we finish this conversation another time? I'm freezing my balls off here."

It came as no surprise when we sat down in the pub later that evening, Freddie and I got some slide-glances from the other patrons. As a newcomer to the village, this would have sent me into a blind panic. Now, I didn't care. If you lived your life so carefully as to not become fodder for the gossips, you may as well not live at all.

The conversation begun with the health of Gladys, the ill client. She was okay, and had already sent word that it hadn't deterred her from returning to Auchtermachen again.

"I guess you want to ask me about Jack, now," Freddie prompted.

I settled in my chair and put down my drink. "I thought I was the only one that knew," I began. "I felt awful. Knowing he was lying to everyone."

"Believe me, when I saw his name online and realised he worked for that shit paper, I was raging," Freddie admitted. "I remember the article they'd ran last time. I thought Jack had left his job before starting at *Fling*."

Freddie told me what he and Jack discussed that evening. I admit I ended up heading home afterwards feeling no better.

I was faced with constant reminders of Jack at work. He had proved popular with his colleagues, and I still heard his name mentioned now and again. The weekends couldn't come quick enough.

But pretty soon there was something to occupy everybody's mind, when the TV crew came to stay.

I hadn't been sure how I'd react to cameras being in the office, but for those two weeks I hid away in my office a lot more. During a phone call, Tessa waltzed in, followed by a cameraman, and mouthed if it was okay to film in here. I shook my head vehemently. They retreated immediately and left me alone.

The crew filmed Pete in the editing suite and asked him a few questions. He grumbled afterwards that since no one else had volunteered to be interviewed, Tessa had pleaded with him..

Farewell drinks were held in the pub on the crew's last day at Highland Fling. Due to the overspill of people, the function room was used. I discovered Highland Fling would be on the local news the day of the documentary broadcast.

"I wonder if they'll speak to anyone here," said Gemma, still glowing from being the only makeup artist interviewed for the programme.

"They should interview you," Pete said, nodding towards me with his empty pint glass.

I shook my head. "Nah, they're better off talking to you. You can plug Haze and Peat Productions."

"Aye, I bet Tessa would just love that," Pete replied, and went to get another drink.

A month later and the documentary was due to be shown on television that evening. Meanwhile a BBC Scotland van had parked up outside the building, ready for a live link during the evening news. A handful of employees had turned up with new haircuts and smarter clothes than usual.

I'd been in charge of greeting the crew and making sure they had everything they needed. When I popped back to my desk to charge my phone, it started ringing. I caught the name on the screen and cancelled the call. Why would he be getting in touch after all these months?

It was agreed that Selena, Tessa and Freddie would on the local news to advertise the Highland Fling documentary. Everyone else congregated in the reception area and watched the news via the screen above the reception desk.

A cheer went up when the screen cut from the cosy studio to the windy exterior of Highland Fling, just yards from where we were watching. As the young female reporter, clad in jeans and a striped top, began her introduction to the live report, my phone buzzed. Meena had sent a good luck message.

I started sending a reply when someone shouted out, above the din: "It's Jack!"

CHAPTER TWENTY-FIVE

I looked up at the screen. It was true. Jack was being interviewed live outside the building. Everyone was busy shushing everyone else. I couldn't hear what was being said until someone turned up the volume. The reporter was speaking to Jack, and now held her microphone towards him..

"No, my attempt at an authentic Scottish accent wasn't great, I'll admit. Thankfully, the writers - fantastic scribes, by the way - wrote my character as English. Now *that* accent I could do."

"The charming bastard," Gemma said wistfully as the reporter giggled.

"Jack, you've recently left *Highland* Fling, but what was it about the job that attracted you in the first place?"

He hesitated. The smile faltering for a moment as he glanced at the camera.

Go on, tell her. Tell her the real reason.

"How long have you got?" Jack asked.

The interviewer laughed, then addressed the camera again. "Obviously many reasons -"

Jack stepped forward. "I mean, if you have time I can tell you the *real* reason I came to Highland Fling. An exclusive, if you're interested."

Oh my god. He wasn't about to...

The interviewer, looking uncertain, frowned at the camera. "I think we need to get back to the studio, so..."

The screen cut to the studio where the newsreader sat slouched in her chair. Realising *she* was now on screen, the woman sat up straight, paused, then looked at someone off-camera. "Actually, we *can* go back live to Auchtermachen. Janine?"

"What's going on?" Gemma asked from beside me. You couldn't hear a feather drop. Everyone watched the screen in silence. My heart raced.

Now the television was showing a surprised Janine, microphone still clamped in hand, utterly confused. Jack remained next to her, waiting patiently. Selena and Tessa stood behind him, matching looks of bemusement on their faces. Freddie patted Jack on the shoulder before stepping back.

"Er, right! Okay! So, Jack, tell the nation the *real* reason you joined Highland Fling." She held the microphone out to him.

"Thanks, Janine." He paused, lowered his gaze to the ground. I held my breath. Was he really going to confess all live on Scottish television?

"I was here working undercover."

"Undercover? Like a detective?" Janine asked, an indulgent smile playing on her lips.

Jack smiled wryly. "No. Like a journalist."

The gasps around me rose in unison. I caught Pete watching me. He mouthed if I was alright. I nodded and focussed on the interview again.

"I work for *The Daily Informer*. Or did up until two weeks ago," Jack added.

The office came alive as people discussed the bombshell. Others tried to shush them so they could listen to Jack.

"Rupert Murray wanted someone to dig up dirt on the company," Jack was saying. "Unearth anything the paper could use for an article. He said he wanted to destroy Highland Fling."

"Why?" Janine asked.

Jack looked Janine in the eye. "You'd better ask his wife."

"His wife? Magda Churlish?"

More gasps rose from the office. Phones appeared; fingers jabbing furiously at the screens.

Jack nodded. "Or soon to be ex-wife. I think she's handed the divorce papers over by now. That's another scoop for you. It's okay. She's already spoken to me."

"Oh my god," said Janine, more to herself than anyone else. Then she stuck a finger to her ear, and paused as if listening to something, or someone. "Okay. I've to ask you, why are you admitting this now?"

"Because I'm sick of writing false, exaggerated articles about good people. Highland Fling is full of good people. Great people." He turned to address Selena and Tessa. "I'm so sorry. I shouldn't have taken on the job in the first place. I shouldn't have messed you around." He faced the camera again. "I would be proud to work here, and I was. I'm sorry I lied to you all."

I bit my lip. Was he going to mention me?

"I *did* write an article about Highland Fling," Jack went on. "But it's not the kind Mr Murray wanted. If anyone is interested, it's up on my blog - *JackJeffersonWrites dot blogisphere.co.uk*. I've even provided a link to the booking page on the company's website. I hope it helps."

The camera panned back out again. Janine seemed lost in thought for a moment. Someone off-screen prompted her, and she started, then raised the microphone to her mouth.

"Well, Jack, thank you for sharing that with us. Can I ask -?"

"Sorry, Janine. I'd love to stay but I've got to be somewhere. Thank you." He nodded once to the camera, and walked off-screen.

Janine returned to face the camera. The screen split as it showed both Janine and the newsreader discussing the revelations. Inside, nobody was watching anymore. Calls were made, the interview dissected and analysed.

He hadn't mentioned me. Not once.

"At least he owned up to what he did," I told Pete as he reached my side.

"I've just read his blog. I think you should, too."

"So he sings our praises," I said, sliding off the edge of the desk. "So what? It doesn't make up for what he did."

"And what *did* he do, Carla?"

"You know what he did."

"Yes, and I know what he didn't do. He didn't write what he was supposed to, did he? He could have done. Could have ripped this company a new one, but he didn't."

"I'm meant to just forgive him, am I?"

"Maybe. He's trying to make amends, though. Isn't that worth something? I know how pissed off you are. You were close and he lied. I get that. He made a mistake."

"Yeah, just a wee one," I said.

"Read his blog. Please? And then maybe reach out to him."

"'Reach out to him'? Since when have you watched Oprah?" My attempt at sarcasm was met with a scowl. But then he winked and left.

With the show over, people disappeared back to wherever they'd been before. I returned to my desk and continued my work. I would get on with my life, now the chapter marked 'Jack Jefferson' had ended.

But as I answered emails and printed out reports, the thought of the blog stayed heavy on my mind. When I found myself typing 'jefferson' instead of 'jeffreys' in an email, I gave in and went to check what Jack had to say for himself.

CHAPTER TWENTY-SIX

A Confession

Dear readers of this blog, I know you've come to expect some jovial (and juvenile) scribings from yours truly, but this time things are a little different.

You see, I'm an idiot.

And before you all rush to agree with me, let me tell you why... And then you can continue to agree with me.

Some of you know that I write 'popcorn' pieces for the Daily Informer. Some of you realise that what I write on my blog is far superior and truer to who I am (thank you for your comments in past posts).

But what none of you know is the amazing, confusing, infuriating couple of months I've just endured.

You see, my boss (I won't name him here, but you can easily google who it is) sent me up to Bonnie Scotland to go undercover. 'Ooh' I hear you say, 'tell us more'. Well, I will.

Before you get settled down, I have to tell you that it wasn't an undercover operation to seek out malpractices at public institutions or the behaviour of staff at a care home.

No, my boss wanted me to go undercover to a perfectly innocent holiday package company, simply because he doesn't like his wife booking them.

Highland Fling is the ideal destination for readers of time travel romances. You book your holiday, and upon arrival find yourself in the highlands of 18th century Scotland, where you encounter a dashing highlander and play out your own romantic story. It's all very chaste and swoon-worthy rather than anything else. The most the client gets is a kiss. And to get a little Big Brother for a moment, your entire stay is recorded by discreet cameras around the small village replica. No, don't worry. This is all above board and mentioned when the client signs up for their stay. The cameras are so that the client can leave with their very own 'movie' of their time travel romance. And for those who are asking "but what about...?" Don't worry. The cameras are always switched off after the last romantic meeting between the client and her Hunk.

So, that is where I've been for the past couple of months, working as a Hunk with a terrible accent.

I hated it, and I loved it. Yes, I went there with the intention to write a hack piece on the place, just to satisfy my boss. But you know what? The people of Highland Fling are doing no harm whatsoever. That's right. I couldn't dig up any dirt on them. And I didn't want to. How could I do it to these people who had found a niche market and went for it? They are just providing a service, which is more than can be said for my ex-employer.

Yes, I've finally listened to my inner voice and all of you, and quit my job in London. It's scary but the overwhelming sense of relief more than makes up for it. And at the risk of virtue signalling, I will just say I never spent any of my Highland Fling wage. It never felt right somehow. So, if there is anyone from Auchtermachen who knows of any local causes I can donate the money to, please get in touch.

So there we go. That's what's been happening in my life for the past wee while (ha, a bit of Scots creeping in there). Now I'm going to continue job hunting. Anybody in need of a journo with a conscience?

CHAPTER TWENTY-SEVEN

I stared at the picture accompanying the post. A selfie taken in The Snug. Jack and I grinning like fools. Happier times. I read the caption underneath: *Me and The Missy.*

I got up and went across to the window. I needed air. My mind was racing, and I didn't know what to do. I moved back to the computer and read the words again.

Edited to Add: Missy, I'm adding this in the hope that you are reading this, and I haven't totally wrecked the one thing I never *lied about during my time in Auchtermachen.*

If there is the slimmest possibility of giving me another chance, call me before 6.35pm. That's when I board the train south and my phone doesn't travel very well.

If not, give my love to Dalek Fred.

I checked the time on the corner of the computer screen. An hour and three quarters until he left Inverness. An hour and three quarters to decide.

There was a knock at the door. If it was Pete with more of his soppy wisdom, I didn't want to hear it. But to my surprise, Gemma walked in. She looked surprised when she saw me.

"What are you still doing here?" she asked.

"I finish at five." I was on my guard. What did she want?

"I don't mean that," she snapped. "Why aren't you with Jack?"

Now it was my turn to be surprised. "What?"

"You've read the blog, I assume?"

"Yeah. So?"

"Jesus, Carla. I thought you liked the guy."

"I *did*."

"You still do. Don't bullshit me by saying otherwise. I know you, Carla Kingston."

"I'm not to go after a man who lied to me. To all of us. He could have really done a number on this place."

Gemma rolled her eyes and made an 'ugh' sound. "Coulda, woulda, shoulda. The fact is, he didn't. He chose not to. It looks like he quit his job instead of writing what his boss wanted him to. Doesn't that count for anything?"

Damn. She *was* right. I *know* she was right. He could have easily done as he'd been told. But he hadn't. He'd walked away, instead.

"What is it with everyone? Have you been talking to Pete?" I said, grumpily.

"About this? Yes, and we're both in agreement; you're just being stubborn and woe-is-me. You fancy him. He, annoyingly, fancies you, too. He's just proved he's less of a jerk than some guys I could mention."

I knew she was referring to Lance. Since we'd stopped talking, I'd not been able to ask her if she'd ever caught up with the ex-heartthrob.

"So, stop being stupid and call him, like he says on his blog," continued Gemma. "Or I'll make you go on umpteen, disastrous double-dates."

"Disastrous?"

"For you, yeah. So, get your phone out and -" said Gemma, before pausing and looking at her watch. "Five o'clock. What time was his train leaving?"

"About half six," I replied, then frowned. "Why?"

When Gemma suddenly grins, it's very worrying. She looked like the Cheshire Cat. "Go to the train station, instead!" she squealed, eyes wide with delight.

"I'm not going to the train station," I laughed.

"Yeah!" she went on, warming to her theme. "God, it'll be like a -"

"Don't say a Richard Curtis movie," I said.

"A Richard Curtis movie!"

A fit of the giggles overcame me. I had to sit down.

Gemma looked bemused. "What did I say?"

A small laugh escaped my mouth, as my eyes leapt back to the photo on the screen. "Oh what the hell," I said, surrendering. "I'll go to the train station."

Gemma fist-pumped the air. "Yes! Atta girl! Let's go now. We'll make it in plenty of time."

"*We'll* make it in plenty of time?" I echoed, shutting down the computer.

"You'll need someone to *not* talk you out of it on the way there," Gemma explained.

I really didn't want her to come along, but at the same time I knew that if I *did* go by myself then I *would* talk myself out of it. I thought about arguing with her, but decided life was too short.

"Fine. Whatever, but are you sure? I mean, won't it be a little awkward?" I asked.

"How do you mean? Because you stole Jack off me?" She asked, then broke out into a grin. "Only kidding. Well, half-kidding. Anyway, are we going to stand here all day or are we off to create a romantic happy ending?"

"Shut up," I smiled, and led the way out.

As we moved through the car park, my keys already in my hand, I noticed a strange man loitering by my car.

"Ah, yes. Forgot about him," I heard Gemma say, as we reached the stranger. "Carla, I said you'd give Ben here a lift to the station. Hope you don't mind."

"You said I'd drop him off at the station, before knowing if I was even going?" I asked her, unlocking the car.

"I knew you would," said Gemma. "So it's okay?" She asked, eyebrows raised.

Dressed in a blue waterproof jacket, khaki cargo shorts and leather walking boots, Ben had the hallmarks of a hiker. The only thing missing was a massive backpack. Instead, a black man bag hung over one shoulder.

"I can get a taxi, if it's a problem," he said, his accent reminding me of Jack and the whole purpose of going to Inverness.

"It's fine," I told them both. "Get in."

Gemma slid into the passenger's seat, while Ben and his bag sat in the back.

As we drove out of the car park and joined the main road, Gemma reached down and switched the radio on, and *Everlasting Love* by Love Affair blasted out of the speakers.

"Oh you can shut up," I said, reaching to turn it off. "I'm not Bridget Jones."

"Leave it on." Gemma batted my hand away. "It's a good song."

Grumbling, I concentrated on driving while my two passengers sang along. By the time we joined the A9, I'd given in and was harmonising to Edison Lighthouse. What if Jack had changed *his* mind since writing his blog post? What if I was wasting my time?

"Nervous?" Gemma asked quietly, when Ben took a call on his phone.

"A bit," I admitted.

"That's cute."

"So," I began, glancing in the rear-view mirror as Ben continued his phone call *sotto voce*. "What's the story with you and...?"

Gemma shrugged. "No story. He's part of the documentary crew, but he's heading northwards for a mini-break."

"And you've not managed to invite yourself along?" I teased.

She considered this for a moment. "Nah. Anyway, I'm not a fan of moustaches."

I looked at the man's reflection again. That was a very busy moustache he was rocking. Akin to something from the heady days of the 1970s. I briefly pictured Jack with similar facial hair, and shuddered.

Normally, the A9 to Inverness was a fairly quiet road. But not that day. Of course, not that day. It seemed everyone had decided to visit the city simultaneously. Twice, we had found ourselves in a tail-back. I checked the time on the dashboard. I still had twenty minutes until the train was due to leave. But that wasn't enough. I didn't know what platform to go to, or how many carriages I'd need to check.

I was about to abort the mission when Gemma, who had been tapping at her phone for the past few minutes, shrieked in my ear.

"Cancelled!" She squealed, then held the phone up to me. Since by then I was concentrating on the road, I could only give it a customary glance. From the brief glimpse I got, she'd been looking at the Scotrail website.

"His train's cancelled?" I asked, a glimmer of hope appearing before me.

Gemma nodded, and then laughed. "A signalling failure somewhere between here and Glasgow. Next train isn't for another two hours! For once, a cancelled train is a good thing!"

"He might get a different train," I said, cynically.

"Hang on, we're being stupid," said Gemma, as we finally reached the outskirts of Inverness. "Why don't we just call him? Less romantic, but at least he'll know."

"I can't use a phone. I'm driving."

"I can."

"You still have his number?"

"Sweetheart, I rarely delete a man's number. You never know. Anyway, shush." She turned the radio down and held the phone to her ear. "Well, it's ringing," she said, after several seconds of silence.

I could feel my heartbeat quicken. The nerves were definitely getting to me, now.

"No answer," Gemma huffed, finally giving up after a full minute. "Maybe he can't hear if he's still in the station."

I shrugged. Maybe it was a sign. A sign I was doing the wrong thing by chasing him.

I said as much to Gemma, even as we drove into the Rose Street car park, the same one Jack and I parked in during our mission to get Pete's present.

"Right, give me your keys," said Gemma. "I'll lock up. You go find Jack."

I tossed the car keys to Gemma and got out. Our quiet passenger was getting out, too, but he didn't seem the type to rush, so I left him as I hurried out of the car park. I hear Gemma yell "Good luck!" after me.

By the time I reached the side of the TK Maxx store on Strothers Lane, I had a stitch in my side and was out of breathe. I nearly collided with someone as I turned onto Academy Street. The woman was leaving M & Co, carrying a bag in one hand and had a phone clamped to her ear She shrieked as I almost knocked her over.

"Sorry!" I hollered, without stopping. I was nearly there. I just hoped Jack was still in the station.

The station was busy, as train stations usually are. I scanned the faces of the people nearby, then, checking the Departures board, discovered I needed to be at Platform 9, and no ¾.

There were half a dozen or so people on the platform when I eventually found it. But not the one I was searching for.

I contemplated looking in nearby bars and cafes, but knew it was futile. I had let the fact he hadn't answered his phone when Gemma tried to call him slide. But I had to face facts sooner or later. He had changed his mind, and gone.

"Excuse me?" A teenage girl with a Black Panther rucksack and a pierced tongue stood next to me. "I think someone wants your attention."

In confusion, I looked to where she was pointing.

Directly opposite, across the track at Platform 8 was Jack. He was in a carriage, looking through the window. His hands clasped in prayer, he was mouthing 'thank you' to the teen.

"Oh, thanks," I said. She shrugged, and walked away.

Jack and I stared at one another for what seemed like forever. Then when I realised he wasn't going to move until I prompted him, I made a beckoning motion with my hand.

Realisation hit him as he laughed and nodded, then got out of his seat and reached to get his luggage from the rack above.

The grin on my face became a look of horror as the train slowly began to move.

CHAPTER TWENTY-NINE

"You have got to be kidding me," I said outloud, to no one in particular, though I did get a strange look from a member of the railway staff. I caught a glimpse of a panic-stricken Jack mouth the *f*-word before his carriage and the train disappeared from sight.

I stood there, at a loss at what to do. Then my phone began to ring. I did ignore it for a moment, then something made me think it was Jack.

It *was* Jack.

"Carla?" He asked, when I hit 'answer'. I bit my tongue, the temptation to say 'obviously' perhaps not necessary.

"Do you think fate is trying to tell us something?" I joked, nervously, as I began to make my way out of the station.

"Fate's over-rated," he declared, then added. "You read my blog, then?"

"Yes."

"But you didn't call me."

"No."

"You came to the station instead."

"Yes, I thought it would be -" I stopped before the word 'romantic' escaped my lips.

"Like a Richard Curtis movie?" He asked, then laughed softly. "I'm glad you did, though I'm sorry it was a wasted journey. I didn't think you would, to be honest. That's why I got this train, when the other one was cancelled. Cost me a small fortune."

"I should have called earlier."

"Doesn't matter. Look, I'm going to get off at the next stop. Head home. I'll try and get back to Auchtermachen somehow."

"You'd better." I said, heading towards the car park. "You're making me breakfast in bed, tomorrow morning."

"Mmm. I like the sound of that -"

There was suddenly silence on the other end. I looked at my screen. The call had been cut short. Jack did say his phone wasn't good travelling.

When I reached the car, Gemma was in the passenger's seat, flicking idly through a social media feed.

"Where is he?" She asked, when I slid in next to her.

" I need you to look up the stops for the Inverness to Edinburgh train," I replied. "Like right now."

As I left my ipso-facto PA to do her research, I drove us out of the car park and through the town.

"Um, Carla?" Gemma looked up from her screen. Her face had taken on a worried look. I had a hunch as to what she was about to say.

"What is it?"

"The next stop *is* Edinburgh." She revealed, then looked at her screen again. "If he'd taken an earlier one then he could have got off at Perth."

"Bugger," I muttered.

"You know," Gemma began. "It's only a couple of hours to Edinburgh. We could probably beat the train."

"It's after half six. It's a bit late to go gallivanting down the country."

"True. But it would be a nice surprise for him to get off the train, thinking all is lost, and then see you there on the platform."

"It would be about ten when we reached Waverley Station," I argued. "You expect me to then drive us all the way back home? Look, it's been a long day."

"Yes, that's why I'm currently looking at available hotels in the city," countered Gemma. "It is Friday, after all."

"I've not got any money on me," I said. That wasn't quite true. I had about thirty pounds in my wallet. Definitely not enough for a hotel room."

My phone began ringing. "Just ignore it," I said, concentrating on the road.

"It might be him," Gemma said, and promptly answered the phone from where it lay in the glove compartment. "I'll put it on loudspeaker. Jack?"

"Carla?" Jack's disrupted voice sounded vague.

"Gemma. Carla's driving at the moment. She can hear you, though."

"Hi, Jack," I said.

"The train's not stopping anywhere until it gets to Edinburgh," he said.

"We know," Gemma and I said in unison.

"I'll find somewhere to sleep tonight, then I'll call you in the morning," he said, and then added. "Preferably without the lovely Gemma listening in."

"Charming," Gemma remarked.

"Okay," I said, ignoring my passenger's pout. "Take care."

The call ended.

"Ugh, I hate it when people don't say goodbye before hanging up," said Gemma, putting my phone back.

"I don't think he intentionally ended the call."

The car came to a stop as we reached a roundabout and heavy traffic.

"So shall we get a bottle of wine and see what's on Netflix?" suggested Gemma. "Since we're not going to the Auld Reekie?"

I didn't answer. I was at a crossroads. Literally. Ahead of us was a sign. The left road would lead us back to the village. The right, eventually Edinburgh. I would be sensible. I would return to Auchtermacher_ and await Jack getting in touch. I'd been awake since 7am, and it had been a long day. Plus, I was hungry and -

I turned right.

Gemma squealed when she realised what this meant.

"Yes! You go, girl!" she whooped.

"Try not deafen me too much, will you?" I replied, switching the radio on as the seven o'clock news report was in mid-flow.

"Like a Mountie, you always get your man," announced Gemma.

"I must be crazy," I murmured, as we joined the flow of traffic heading along the A9.

"Crazy in love!" Gemma remarked, before proceeding to sing the Beyonce classic.

Could I put up with this for the next four hours?

By the time we crossed the Forth Bridge, the dazzling lights of the Scottish capital before us, I was proud that I hadn't resorted to killing Gemma, despite her doing likewise to almost every song that played on the radio. In fact, I'd been singing along with her, murdering the classics since we passed through Dunkeld. But now it was 10 pm and lethargy was setting in. The radio volume was low, the windows were down a little to let in some fresh air, and there was a silence between us.

Gemma had ended up booking a room for the night, with the reassurance that she would be staying with a friend. The gender not forthcoming.

At last the train came into view. All ten carriages. Jack had been on the second carriage, as far as I remembered, but the train passed so quickly, the figures inside were a blur. I moved down the platform, so he'd see me when the doors opened. There were a crowd of people waiting to get on, so I moved back, concerned that we'd miss one another.

Finally I saw him. He weaved through the crowd towards me, and I felt the nerves visit. He stopped right in front of me, but he hadn't noticed me. Instead, he was busy tapping the screen on his phone.

I leant forward, so he could hear. "If you're texting me, don't waste your money."

He glanced up with a frown. Then he laughed in surprise. "What the hell? Didn't I just see you in Inverness?"

"Several hours ago, yes." I told him.

"You came all this way? You're crazy."

"I know."

"I'm glad, though," Jack went on. He went to say more, but the mass of people around us was getting bigger. "Let's get out of here, eh?"

"Gladly."

We headed out of the train station and found ourselves on the corner of Princes Street. Rain sparkled against the soft glow of the street lights. Even at this time of night, the city was alive.

"I take it you forgive me," said Jack, as we moved out of the way of a stream of people heading in and out of the station steps.

"Would I be here if I hadn't?" I said.

"We *have* just established that you're crazy. Anything is possible."

I grinned. "Follow me." I tried not to smile too much as I stopped a few steps away, and glanced up at the imposing, regal and *expensive* Balmoral Hotel that straddled Princes St and South Bridge. Jack followed my gaze.

"You haven't - ' he began, breaking into a grin.

"No, not me. Gemma. I don't know how she wangled it, but we're staying here for the night."

I moved to go inside but Jack took hold of my arm. "You're definitely crazy. Crazy and wonderful. But mainly crazy. And I need to kiss you right now. I'm having withdrawal symptoms."

"Ah, but it's raining. And if we kiss in the rain, it'd just be a cliché." Truth be told, I was dying to kiss him too, but I was being restraint.

"Hmm, boy meets girl. Boy sleeps with girl. Boy works with girl. Boy balls-up. Boy loses girl. Boy gets girl again. Isn't that a cliché?"

"I'd like to think it's more a case of the girl meets, the girl sleeps, the girl decides to forgive the absolute ass-hat boy for cocking things up."

"In that case, the ass-hat boy is eternally grateful." He did a little bow.

"Not forgetting the final scene where the girl begins re-thinking her decision because the boy won't follow her into the posh hotel."

He saluted. "Yes, miss."

I'd started walking towards the hotel again, but lost my re-straint. I pushed him against the railing next to the road, and sought his mouth.

We only came up for air when someone wolf-whistled nearby.

"Get a room," a young lad in a burberry cap and jogging bottoms muttered as he passed us.

"Oh, we're going to," I called out after him, and led my Highland Heartthrob towards the hotel.

Epilogue

So, there you go. That's my own romance story, though not quite reaching the farcical heights of a Richard Curtis movie. Jack is no Hugh Grant, but then again I'm hardly Andie Mac-Dowell or Julia Roberts. I'm much more of a Bridget Jones-type anyway - I have a drawer full of big pants to prove it.

You'll want to know what happened after Jack and I entered the hotel. I'll leave *that* to your imaginations but a year later we are still together. Bickering and bantering in Auchtermachen. I still work for Highland Fling, but I'm looking to spread my wings.

Jack received a bit of attention after his blog post and revelations during the live news broadcast. He's gone freelance, writing guest articles for various journals and websites. He also works at The Thistled Inn, most nights. His income is a lot less than what he'd been getting, but he says his mental health appreciates it.

Haze & Peat Productions is officially two months old! Hazel and Pete quit their jobs to focus on their company full time. I lend a hand at the weekends when I can. Their first completed short film, on the history of Scotland in literature, will be shown on BBC4 later in the year.

Last but not least, Gemma has shocked everyone by not only settling down, but getting married! Remember Ben, the guy we gave a lift to on our way to the train station to find Jack? Well, he came back to the village, *sans* moustache, and swept her off her feet. After the wedding, they settled just south of Edinburgh. We keep in touch and Jack and I are travelling down to spend Christmas with them.

So, if you're ever in Auchtermachen, pop in and say hello. Stay for a while. Who knows, you may just find your own highland heartthrob...

Did you love *Highland Fling*? Then you should read *The Twin Dilemma* by Izzy Hunter!

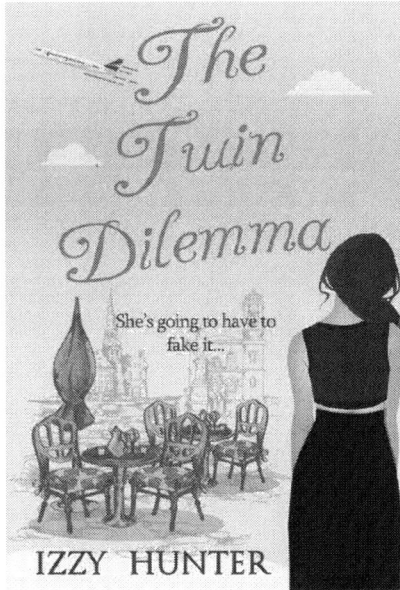

My twin's just stolen my life.Armed with my luggage, money and passport, Jen's ran away to the airport and it's too late to catch her.Now her boyfriend's turned up and - guess what? - he thinks I'm Jen!I could protest. I could stay in my lonely flat and sulk while my sister lives it up in Las Vegas for the next few weeks.Or maybe I could use this situation to my advantage.My name is Sara. My twin's just stolen my life. Now it's payback time.

Also by Izzy Hunter

Curiosity Killed (A Short Story Fantasy)
A Town Called No Hope
The Twin Dilemma
Loving the Alien
Highland Fling

Printed in Great Britain
by Amazon